James Munro

A New Gaelic Primer

Containing elements of pronunciation, an abridged grammar, formation of

words, a list of Gaelic and Welsh vocables of like signification. Third

Edition

James Munro

A New Gaelic Primer
*Containing elements of pronunciation, an abridged grammar, formation of words, a
list of Gaelic and Welsh vocables of like signification. Third Edition*

ISBN/EAN: 9783337406905

Printed in Europe, USA, Canada, Australia, Japan

Cover: Foto ©Andreas Hilbeck / pixelio.de

More available books at **www.hansebooks.com**

A NEW
GAELIC PRIMER:

CONTAINING

ELEMENTS OF PRONUNCIATION; AN ABRIDGED GRAMMAR;
FORMATION OF WORDS; A LIST OF GAELIC AND WELSH
VOCABLES OF LIKE SIGNIFICATION:

ALSO,

A COPIOUS VOCABULARY,

WITH

A FIGURED ORTHOEPY; AND A CHOICE SELECTION OF
COLLOQUIAL PHRASES ON VARIOUS SUBJECTS,

HAVING THE PRONUNCIATION MARKED THROUGHOUT

By JAMES MUNRO, H.M.E.I.; I.C.; & O.S.G. &c.

THIRD EDITION,

IMPROVED AND ENLARGED.

EDINBURGH:
MACLACHLAN & STEWART.
LONDON: SIMPKIN, MARSHALL, & CO.

MDCCCLXII.

PREFACE.

The Publishers, and many others, having urged me to superintend a New Edition of this little Manual, I have complied with their request as quickly as my other avocations would permit me.

I have increased, and tried to make the matter of the book as simple and clear as I could; and I hope that those who may feel disposed to study Gaelic will, on a fair trial, find this Primer of considerable advantage.

J. M.

January 1854.

INDEX.

	Page
Accidents,	34
Adjectives,	15, 70
Agriculture.	45
Animals,	52
Apparel,	38, 39
Astronomy,	49
Birds,	52
Body, of the	31
Church, of a	42
Coins,	58
Colours,	27
Commerce,	43
Comparison of Adjectives,	15
Do. of Gaelic and Welsh,	20
Days of the Week,	28
Declension,	12
Diseases,	33
Division of Year,	28
Earth, of the	50
Elements,	26
Faculties of Body,	33
Fire,	51
Fishes,	53
Food and Drink,	37
Formation of Words,	19
Fruits,	46
Geography,	49
House, of a	40
Implements,	44
Insects,	55
Kindred,	30
Key to Sounds,	24
Mankind, of	29
Measures,	57, 58

		Page
Metals,		48
Mind, of the		35
Music,		49
Names,		56, 59
Numbers,		60
Passive Voice,		19
Peculiar Sounds,		10
Phraseology,		68
Pronouns,		63
Pronunciation,		1
Questions,		84
Reptiles,		54
Rural Affairs,		44
Seasonings,		38
States of Europe,		55
Terms and Holidays,		29
Time,		28
Titles,		57
Town, of a		41, 56
Trades,		43
Vegetables,		47
Vegetation,		48
Verbs,		/ 6, 64
Vices,		36
Virtues,		35
Vocabulary,		26
Water,		58
Weights,		51

ERRATA.

Page 1, line 7 from top, insert *ph* between mh and sh.
„ 42, line 9 from top, dele *g* in fuigni, and pronounce foŏni.
„ 48, line 2 from top, dele *comma* after croabh, and read craobh.
„ 54, line 16 from top, for muirsginn, read muirsginn.
„ 69, line 6 from top, dele *The Articles.*
„ 70, line 5 from top, for mèirleach, read mòirleach.
„ 73, line 3 from bottom, mid. col. for tŭsh, read tûsh.

GAELIC PRIMER.

The Alphabet consists of eighteen letters :—
Vowels, a, e, i, o, u ;
Consonants, b, c, d, f, g, h, l, m, n, p, r, s, t.
a, o, u, are called *broad* vowels.
e, i, are called *small* vowels.
bh, ch, dh, fh, gh, mh, sh, th, are called aspirates.

c, d, g, l, n, r, s, t, are termed linguals; b, bh, f, m, p, labials ; m, n, mh, nasals.

The various powers of each and all of these letters and combinations are fully explained and exemplified in the Introduction to the Vocabulary.

PRONUNCIATION.

MONOSYLLABLES.

1.   ă as *a* in hăt, făt.

ab, *shame*	can, *sing*
bab, *a tuft*	fan, *wait*
pab, *crumple*	cas, *steep*, &c.
ad, *a hat*	las, *kindle*
fad, *length*	car, *a turn*
lag, *weak*, &c.	gar, *warm* (v.)
rag, *stiff*	cat, *a cat*
gal, *weeping*	as, *out of*
sal, *dirt*	bas, *a palm*

2.   à as *a* in tàr, fár.

càl, *kail*	bàn, *fair*
màl, *rent*	làn, *full*
ràn, *a roar*	àm, *time*
làr, *ground*	làd, *a load*
bàs, *death*	fàd, *a peat*

---

3.   ea like *a* in late, kate.*

fead, *a whistle*	breab, *a kick*
cead, *leave*	eas, *a waterfall*
beag, *little*	eag, *a notch*
deas, *south*	teas, *heat*

---

4.   so also ei, as

ceil, *conceal*	geir, *tallow*
deil, *a spindle*	speir, *a shank*
meil, *grind*	beir, *bear*

---

5.   i as in sin, *it*, did.

bil, *a lip*	min, *meal*
fir, *men*	big, *little ones*

---

6.   so io, in

fios, *notice*	lios, *a garden*
cion, *want*	mion, *minute* (a.)

---

7.   ì like ie in field.

bìd, *a chirp*	dìg, *a ditch*
ìm, *butter*	mìn, *smooth*

---

8.   so ìo, in

stìom *a fillet*	plòb, *a pipe*
fìon, *wine*	sìon, *weather*

---

9.   o like o in pot, sod.

Rob, *Robert*	dod, *dumps*

---

* As generally pronounced in the Lowlands.

dog, *a junk* dol, *going*
cor, *condition* cos, *a foot*

---

10. ò like o in córd, stórk.

pòg, *a kiss* òrd, *a hammer*
còrr, *remainder* mòr, *large*
ròp, *a rope* tòn, *a bottom*
còir, *a right* fòil, *quiet, still*
mòid, *greatness.* fòir, *help, aid*

---

11. ù as u in trŭc, crŭdc.

dùn, *a heap* dùr, *stubborn*
tùr, *sense* tùm, *dip*
smùid, *smoke* cùis, *a matter*
sùil, *an eye* brùid, *a brute*

---

12. On bl, cl, fl, br, cr, fr, &c.

blas, *taste* gràn, *grain*
crag, *a rock* gràp, *a grape*
bran, *a dog's name* gràs, *grace*
srad, *a spark* trà, *a time*
crcid, *believe* crios, *a belt*
gliog, *a jingle* clod, *a clod*
spiol, *pluck* smid, *a syllable*

àrc, *a cork* alt, *a joint* .
àrd, *high* faisg, *nigh*
fàisg, *squeeze* mort, *murder*
puist, *posts* bràisd, *a brooch*
calg, *awn* plosg, *a pant*

---

13. s sounds ss, or s hard, in the same syllable with
a, o, u.

bas, *a palm* sad, *dust*
tòs, *also* sop, *a straw*
tùs, *beginning* sult, *fatness*

14. s sounds *sh* (as in *she*) in the same syllable with *e* or *i*.

séud, *a jewel*	ccis, *a creel*
séinn, *sing*	cùis, *a matter*
*seas, *stand*	crois, *a cross*
sìol, *seed*	créis, *grease*
siap, *sneak*	clais, *a furrow*
siar, *west*	leisg, *laziness.*

---

15. On t, d,—c, g,—p, b.

tà, *is, are*	pab, *rumple*
dà, *two*	bab, *a tuft*
tuit, *fall*	prat, *a trick*
duit, *to thee*	brat, *a covering*
car, *a turn*	bìnn, *melodious*
gar, *warm,* (*v.*)	pìnn, *pens.*

---

16. Final c, in many words, is pronounced chq.

mac, *a son*	cearc, *a hen*
bac, *hinder*	torc, *a boar*
soc, *a snout*	muc, *a sow*
boc, *a buck*	leac, *a flag*
olc, *bad*	malc, *rot*
pluic, *a cheek*	àirc, *an ark*
&c.	&c.

---

17. chd final sounds chq.

achd, *manner*	iochd, *pity, ruth*
ochd, *eight*	bochd, *poor*
uchd, *a breast*	tachd, *suffocate*
seachd, *seven*	smachd, *control*
&c.	&c.

---

* Sound *shÿess*.

18.   final g sounds q, as in que, *Fr.*

glag, *a noise*   spòg, *a paw*
spliug, *a bubble,* &c.   eag, *a notch*
diog, *a syllable*   aog, *death.*

_____

final g preceded by *i,* sounds k.

smig, *a chin*   leig, *permit*
snàig, *creep*   mùig, *gloom.*

_____

19. The broad and small vowels have a similar power
over c, d, g, l, n, r, s,* t.

_____

20.   On bh, ch, dh, &c. called aspirate consonants.

bh sounds like v, in vote, give.
ch   —   — ch in lo*ch*, or gh in cou*gh*.†
dh   —   — y in *y*e, before or after e, i;
and   —   — r in bu*r*, as uttered in Northumber-
land, before or after a, o, u.
fh is mute.
gh sounds like dh.
mh   —   — bh, only more nasal.
ph   —   — f in *f*oe, *f*ine.
sh   —   — h in *h*e, *h*ad.
th   —   — h in *h*oe, *h*ave.

_____

ÉXAMPLES.

bhà, *was, were*
bhos, *on this side*   sàbh, *a saw*
bhac, *did hinder*   éubh, *a cry*
bhris, *did break*   deilbh, *warp,* (v.)
dròbh, *a drove*   balbh, *dumb*
chroch, *did hang*   deich, *ten*
chlisg, *did start*   faich, *a plain.*

_____

chrom, *did bend*

chlos, *did rest*

dhòirt, *did spill*

dhùisg, *did awake*

dh'éisd, *did listen*

fhliuch, *did wet*

fhrois, *did shower*

*dh'fhan, *did wait*

dh'fhàisg, *did squeeze*

ghlan, *did clean*

ghreas, *did hurry*

ghlais, *did lock*

mhùth, *did change*

mhort, *did murder*

mhath, *did forgive*

phòs, *did marry*

pheasg, *did chap*

shil, *did drop*

shéid, *did blow*

sheirm, *did ring*

tha, *is, are*

thog, *did lift*

thig, *will come*

cluich, *play*

troich, *a dwarf*

bìdh, *of food*

suidh, *sit (v.)*

cràdh, *pain*

fhlùr, *of flowers*

fhleasg, *of garlands*

dh'fhuin, *did knead*

*m'fhalt, *my hair*

plàigh, *a plague*

dòigh, *a mode*

meigh, *a balance*

nimh, *poison*

nèamh, *heaven*

sàimh, *luxury*

phìll, *did return*

phlosg, *did pant*

shaill, *did salt*

sheas, *did stand*

shluig, *did swallow*

crath, *shake*

sruth, *a stream*

srath, *a strath.*

21.   Peculiar Vowel-Sounds.

a sounds like e in her, or i in bird, in

a', am, an, *the*

a, *who, which*

magh, *a field (moy)*

blagh, *sense*

---

* Suppress fh in reading, and substitute the dh' in its place; thus, dhăn, dhàisg, malt, &c.

agh, *a heifer*
lagh, *law*
   &c.

dragh, *trouble*
ma, *if*
   &c.

---

22.   Final *a** and final *e*, in dissyllables, sounds *uh,* u being as in gun, must: as,

àra, *f. a kidney*
bar'a, *m. a barrow*
cas'a, *f. feet*
dor'ra, *a. worse*
gior'ra, *a. shorter*
bil'e, *m. a rim*
cail'e, *f. a girl*
duill'e, *m. a sheath*
eil'e, *other*
fàil'e, *m. scent*

lìon'ta, *m. nets*
measg'ta, *a. mixed*
nàr'a, *a. shameful*
or'ra, *on them*
pòs'ta, *married*
gil'e, *f. whiteness*
làin'e, *f. fulness*
min'e, *f. of meal*
nis'e, *now*
oir're, *on her.*

---

23.   The combination ao represents the prolonged sound of *u* in f*u*n, m*u*st, *i* in s*i*r, *e* in h*e*r, or *o* in s*o*me, &c.

aois, *f. age*
baois, *f. folly*
†caob, *m. a clod*
daor, *a. dear*
†faob, *m. a lump*

gaol, *m. love*
laogh, *m. a calf*
†maor, *m. a messenger (mayor)*
plaosg, *m. a husk,* &c.
†raon, *m. a field.*

---

24.   ua is made up of *u* in p*u*t, and *a* in *a*t.

bruach, *f. a bank*
cuach, *f. a cup*

guad, *m. a wile*
luan, *m. a lamb*

---

* Final *a* sounds uh in -ad, -ead, -ach, -adh, -amh, -eamh, -ar, -as, &c.: as, ur'ad, *as much;* moill'ead, *slowness;* aod'ach, *cloth;* far'adh, *a ladder;* deanamh, *doing;* calamh, *quick;* eab'ar, *puddle,* &c.

† Caob, shortened, would be pronounced *cup;* faob, *fup;* maor, *mur;* raon, *run,* &c. By inverting the process—*i.e.,* lengthening the pronunciation of mur—you arrive at maor; and so of the rest.

dual, *m. a plait*	guail, *m. of coal*
fuar, *a. cold*	sguain, *f. rigmarole.*

---

25. n, after c, g, m, is sometimes improperly sounded like *r :* as,

cnac, *f. a knock*	mnà, *f. of a woman*
cnò, *f. a nut*	mnaoi, *to a woman*
gnos, *m. a snout*	cnoc, *m. a knoll.*

---

26. ·   DECLENSION.

1. Cat, *m. a cat.*

	Sing.	*Plur.*	So, saor, *m. a joiner*
N. & Ac.	cat	cait	maor, *m. a messenger*
G.	cait	chat	craos, *m. a wide mouth*
D.	cat	cataibh	bàrd, *m. a poet*
V.	a chait	a chata	laoch, *m. a hero.*

---

2. Càrnn, *m. a heap of stones.*

N. & Ac.	càrnn	cùirnn	So, dòrnn, *m. a fist*
G.	cùirnn	chàrnn	ceòl, *m. music*
D.	càrnn	càrnnaibh	seòl, *m. a sail*
V.	a chùirnn	a chàrnna	dos, *m. a tuft.*

---

3. Dall, *m. a blind person.*

N.	dall	doill	So, Gall, *m. a Lowlander*
G.	doill	dhall	rann, *m. a rhyme*
D.	dall	dallaibh	crann, *m. a mast.*
V.	a dhoill	a dhalla	

Preas, *m. a bush,* &c.

N.	preas	pris	So, ceann, *m. a head*
G.	pris	phreas	meann, *m. a kid*
D.	preas	preasaibh	peann, *m. a pen*
V.	a phris	a phreasa	meall, *m. a bump, lump.*

13

Meur, *m. a finger.*

	Sing.	Plur.
N.	meur	meòir
G.	meòir	mheur
D.	meur	meuraibh
V.	a mheòir	a mheura

So, deur, *m. a drop*
eun, *m. a bird.*
beul, *m. a mouth*
neul, *m. a cloud.*

Fiadh, *m. a deer.*

N.	fiadh	féidh
G.	féidh	fhiadh
D.	fiadh	fiadhaibh
V.	*'fhéidh	*'fhiadha

So, bian, *m. a skin* or *fur*
sliabh, *m. a moor, hill*
dealg, *m. a spindle.*

Lìon, *m. a net.*

N.	lìon	lìn
G.	lìn	lìon
D.	lìon	lìonaibh
V.	a lìn	a lìona

So, sìol, *m. seed*
bachd, *m. a bend;* uchd,
m. a breast.

Nouns in *idh, air, th, a, e,* are the *same* in the sing. cases, and form their plur. by adding *an:* as, bachd*an,* uchd*an,* baillidhe*an, baillies,* dorsaire*an, door-keepers,* gath*an, beams,* &c.

27. FEMININES.

Cearc, *f. a hen.*

	Sing.	Plur.
N.	cearc	cearcan
G.	circe	chearc
D.	cearc	cearcaibh
V.	a chearc	a chearca

So, cròg, *f. an open hand,* g. cròige; bròg, bròige, *a shoe;* crag, *a rock;* craige; spàg, *a claw,* spàige, &c.

* The vocative *a* is suppressed before fh, or a vowel, and an apostrophe inserted instead.

B

28. NOUNS WITH THE ARTICLE.

am bus, *m. the mouth.*

Sing.	*Plur.*
N. *am* bus	*na* buis
G. *a'* bhuis	*nam* bus
D. * $\left.{a' \atop 'n}\right\}$ bhus	*na* busaibh.

---

a' chas, *f. the foot.*

N. *a'* chas	*na* casan
G. *na* coise	*nan* cas
D. $\left.{a' \atop 'n}\right\}$ chois	*na* casaibh.

---

an duine, *m. the man.*

N. *an* duine	*na* daoine
G. *an* duine	*nan* daoine
D. $\left.{an \atop 'n}\right\}$ duine	*na* daoinibh.

---

an saor, *m. the joiner.*

N. an saor	na saoir
G. †an t-saoir	nan saor
D. $\left.{'n \atop an}\right\}$ t-saor	na saoraibh.

---

an t-sùil, *f. the eye.*

N. ‡ an t-sùil	na sùilean
G. na sùla	nan sùl
D. ‡ $\left.{an \atop 'n}\right\}$ t-sùil	na sùilibh.

---

* 'n is contracted for *an* after a preposition ending in a vowel: as, do 'n bhus, for do an bhus.

† t- is put to the gen. and dat. to prevent ambiguity; for, an saor would signify *the* wright, or *their* wright, without the t-.

‡ an sùil would mean *their* eye; t- is used to mark the necessary distinction.

29. ADJECTIVES

are declined like nouns of the same form: as,

maor daor, *m. a dear messenger.*

Sing.	*Plur.*
N. maor daor	maoir dhaora
G. maoir dhaoir	mhaor daora
D. maor daor	maoraibh daora
V. a mhaoir dhaoir	a mhaora daora.

With the article

am maor daor.

N. am maor daor	na maoir dhaora
G. a' mhaoir dhaoir	nam maor daora
D. $\left.\begin{array}{c} a' \\ 'n \end{array}\right\}$ mhaor dhaor	na maoraibh daora.

cearc bhreac, *f. a speckled hen.*

N. cearc bhreac	cearcan breaca
G. circe brice	chearcan breaca
D. circ bhric	cearcaibh breaca
V. a chearc bhreac	a chearca breaca.

ploc odhar, *m. a dun clod.*

N. ploc odhar	pluic ódhra
G. pluic idhir	phloc ódhra
D. ploc odhar	plocaibh ódhra
V. a phluic idhir!	a phloca ódhra!

30. COMPARISON.

The comparative degree is like the gen. sing. femi-nine: as, daoire, brice, idhre,—so, glaise, *grayer;* làine, *fuller;* mìne, *smoother;* bàine, *fairer;* ciùine, *milder,* &c.

Examples of its use.

Is *daoire* each na caora.	A horse is dearer than a sheep.
Bha 'n dé na b' *fhuaire* na'n diugh.	Yesterday was colder than to-day.
Bu taine na pàipeir e.	It was thinner than paper.

---

31. Another form of comparative is formed from the above, in *id:* as, àirdid, bàinid, deirgid; and another from these, in ad, or ead: as,

Is glain*id* e sud.	It is the cleaner for you.
Bu thruim*id* e 'n còrr.	'Twould be the heavier for more.
Cha bhòi'chid e sid, nì.	It is not any the prettier for you.
Tha na neòil a' dol an truim*ead*.	The clouds are becoming heavier, (gloomier).
Tha gach nì 'dol 'an daoir-*ead*.	Everything is growing dearer.

---

32. VERBS.

Is mi, *it is I*, or *I am*, &c.

INDICATIVE MOOD.

Present Tense.	Past Tense.
Sing.	*Sing.*
1. *Is mi, *it is I*	1. *Bu mhi, *it was I*
2. Is tu, *it is thou*	2. Bu tu, *it was thou*
3. Is e, *it is he*	3. B'è, *it was he*
Plur.	*Plur.*
1. Is sinn, *it is we*	1. Bu sinn, *it was we*
2. Is sibh, *it is you*	2. Bu sibh, *it was you*
3. Is iad, *it is they*	3. B' iad, *it was they.*

---

* Is sounds us, and bu sounds boo (short).

The VERB bì, be.

Imperative Mood.

Sing.
1. bitheam — let me be
2. bi — be thou
3. bitheadh e — let him be

Plur.
1. bitheamaid — let us be
2. bithibh — be ye
3. bitheadh iad. — let them be.

INDICATIVE.

Present.

Sing.
1. Ta mi — *I am*
2. Ta thu — thou art
3. Ta e — he is

Plur.
1. Ta sinn — we are
2. Ta sibh — you are
3. Ta iad. — they are.

PAST TENSE.

Bha *mi, &c. — *I was*, &c.

FUTURE TENSE.

Bithidh *mi, &c. — *I shall or will be*, &c.

POTENTIAL MOOD.

Past Tense.

Bhithinn — I might or could be
Bhitheadh tu — thou mightst or couldst be
Bhitheadh e — he might or could be
Bhitheamaid — we might or could be
Bhitheadh sibh — you might or could be
Bhitheadh iad. — they might or could be.

INFINITIVE.—a bhi, to be.

* Repeat the pronouns after *bha* and bithidh, as above, in the present. These specimens exhibit the verb in its simplest aspect. Questions are asked thus; *Am* mi? Is it I? An *robh?* was I? Negations are made thus : *cha* mhi, It is not I ; cha *robh*, I was not. See Grammar for a more extended view. Our limits are here confined.

B 2

Tùm, to dip.

ACTIVE VOICE.

Present Imperative.

Sing.
- 1. Tum*am* — let me dip
- 2. Tum — dip thou
- 3. Tum*adh* e — let him dip

Plur.
- 1. Tum*amaid* — let us dip
- 2. Tum*aibh* — dip ye
- 3. Tum*adh* iad. — let them dip.

PAST INDICATIVE.

*Thum mi	I dipped
Thum thu	thou dippedst
Thum e	he dipped
Thum sinn	we dipped
Thum sibh	you dipped
Thum iad.	they dipped.

FUTURE.

Tumaidh mi, &c.

PAST POTENTIAL.

Sing.
- 1. Thum*ainn* — *I might or could dip*
- 2. Thum*adh* tu — *thou mightst or couldst dip*
- 3. Thum*adh* e — *he might or could dip*

Plur.
- 1. Thum*amaid* — *we might or could dip*
- 2. Thumadh sibh — *you might or could dip*
- 3. Thumadh iad. — *they might or could dip.*

INFINITIVE.

do
a } Thum*adh*, to dip.

---

* Pronounce hoom me, oo, ay, sheen, sheev, eütt.

PASSIVE VOICE.
Imperative.

Tuma*r* *mi, thu, e ; sinn, sibh, iad.

PAST INDICATIVE.

Thum*adh* *mi, &c. *I was dipped.*

FUTURE.

Tuma*r* *mi, &c.

PAST POTENTIAL.

Thum*tadh* *mi, &c. *I should be dipped.*

PAST PARTICIPLE.

†Tum*ta*, dipped.

34. The particle "ag," placed before the infinitive, translates the English active participle in *ing;* as ag éirigh, *rising*, ag innscadh, *telling*, &c. Before a consonant ag becomes a' ; as, a' tumadh, *dipping*, a' càradh, *mending.*

---

35.   FORMATION OF WORDS.

flùr-*ach*, flower*y*	lon'ach, greed*y*
mos-*ach*, nast*y*	sal'ach, dirt*y*
nàr-*ach*, shame*ful*	góbh'lac*h*, fork*ed*
gob'*ach*, beak*ed*.	ròm'*ach*, hair*y*.

---

gar'*adh*, a warm*ing*	séid'eadh, a blow*ing*
las'adh, a kindl*ing*	till'cadh, a return
pòs'adh, a marr*iage*.	mùch'adh, suffoca*tion*.

---

cearc'*ag*, a *little* hen	pis'eag, a kitten
sùil'eag, *a little* eye.	cail'eag, *a little* girl.

cop'*an*, a *small* cup	scirc'ean, a *little* darling
alld'an, a brook*let*.	buic'ean, a *young* buck.

---

* Repeat the pronouns after each change of the verbal form, as on last page.

† Or, according to the general pronunciation, tùm-*te*.

buailt'ear, a thresher
òig'ear, a young *man*.

port-*air*, a ferry*man*
pòit'ear, a drinke*r*.

tùr'*ail*, sens*ible*
dragh'ail, trouble*some*
prìs'cil, precio*us*.

brùid'cil, brut*ish*
cron'ail, hurt*ful*
tàir'cil, disgrace*ful*.

bòid'*ich*, *make* a vow
cuid'ich, *give* help, (aid)
goirt'ich, *make* sore, (hurt)

tiorm'a*ich*, *make* dry
cois'ich, use the feet, (walk)
cron'aich, find fault with, (rebuke)

pàirt'ich, *im*part
&c.

mionn'aich, *make* oath, &c. (swear)

---

36.   Comparison of Gaelic and Welsh.

Gaelic.	*Welsh.*	*English.*
abar,*	aber,	a confluence
achanaich, *entreaty*,	{ achan,	a hymn or chant
	{ achwyn,	a complaint
ath, again, re,	ad,	re, again
ath-liobh, revarnish,	adliw,	a varnish, retint
ath-loisg reburn,	adlosgi,	burn again
ath-fhios, a 2d notice,	adwys,	second summons
aidich, own,	adef,	acknowledge
àl, young brood,	ael, àl,	produce, brood
àr, slaughter,	aer,	slaughter
abhull, appletree	*afal,	an apple
†abhuinn, a river,	*afon,	a river
eag, a notch,	ag,	an opening, cleft
fagus, near,	agaws,	near
cile, other,	aill,	other
calaidh, music,	alaw,	music
aillt, a cliff,	allt,	a cliff
ealamh, quick,	*alaf,	expert

---

* When the Gaelic word is not *Englished*, its signification is the same as in Welsh.

† f in Welsh sounds *v*, bh and mh in Gaelic sound *v*.

Gaelic.	Welsh.	English.
timchioll,	amgylch,	a circuit
iomradh, a rumour,	amrod,	a going round
iomriasan,	amryson,	contention
aimsir,	amser,	time, season
anail,	{ anadyl, anal,	breath
ainneamh,	anaf,	a blemish
an-aimsir, bad weather,	anamser,	unmeet time
an-àireamh,	aneirif,	innumerable
an-mhilis, not sweet,	anfelys,	not sweet
ànrath,	anrhaith,	distress
ar, plough,	ar,	ploughland
air, on,	ar,	on
àrd-dorus,	arddrws,	door lintel
aisinn,	asen,	a rib
à, ath	au,	the liver
beag,	bach,	little
bàta,	bâd,	a boat
baguid,	bagad,	a cluster
bachal,	bagyl,	a crook
baile,	balc,	a balk
plaosg, blaosg,	ballasg,	a husk
bàrd,	*bardd,	a poet
bàthadh,	*bawdd,	a drowning
beithe,	bedw,	birch
bean,	benw,	a woman
bior,	ber,	a spit, &c.
speir,	bèr,	a shank, leg
beairt-each, rich	berth,	rich
bò-thigh,	beudy,	a cowhouse
biodag, a dirk,	bidawg,	a hanger
blas,	blas,	taste
blonag, fat,	{ blawn, bloneg,	fat grease, lard

* Pronounced barth, bawth.

Gaelic.	Welsh.	English.
blàr,	blawr,	hoary
bliochd,	blith,	milk
bliadhna,	blynedd,	a year
bolgan, a leather bag,	bolgan,	a budget
bonn, a base, sole,	bôn,	a base
bréun,	braen,	rotten
braich,	brâg,	malt
breac, motley, pox,	{ braith, brêch,	variegated pox
brù, a belly,	bru,	the womb
bruinne, a breast,	bron,	a breast
bò, a cow,	bu,	kine
bu, was,	bu,	was
buaidh, victory,	budd,	gain
bo-ghille, a cow-boy,	bugail,	a herdsman
bo-ruidheach, (buarach), } a cow-fetter,	burwy,	a cowfetter
bus, a lip, lips,	bus,	the human lip
bodha, a bow, arch,	bwa,	a bow, arch
buthaman, a dolt,	bwhwman,	fluctuation
bùth, a tent; both, a hut,	bwth,	a hut
boit, bait, biadh, food,	bwyd,	food
bodhar,	byddar,	deaf
buidhionn,	byddin,	a band, troop
bil, lip, brim,	byl,	brim, edge
beò, alive,	byw,	alive
cac,	cach,	ordure
cath,	câd,	a battle
caithir, city,	} cadair, caer,	seat of presidency a city
caoin, clear, bright,	cain,	bright, clear
cam,	cam,	crooked
can,	canu,	sing
càr, related,	câr,	a relation
càrnn,	càrn,	a heap

Gaelic.	Welsh.	English.
ceòl, music,	cathyl,	a melody
cabar,	ceber,	a rafter
giomach,	ceimwch	a lobster
coirc,	ceirch,	oats
calbh,	celff,	a pillar
cuileann, holly,	celyn,	a holly wood
carbad,	cerbyd,	a chariot
cèaird, trade, art,	cerdd,	art, craft
geobha, a gulf,	ceufa,	a gulph
ceigeach, fleshy,	cîg,	flesh
cladh,a trench; to spawn,	cludd,	a trench
cloch, a stone,	clog,	a large stone
cnuac,	cnwc,	a bump, lump
tìr, land,	daer,	earth, land
dàil, delay,	dàl,	a stop
darach, oak,	dâr,	an oak
dòrn, a piece,	darn,	a piece
tairgeanadh,	darogan,	a prediction
dais, a heap,	dâs,	a heap
déug, ten,	dêg,	ten
è,	e,	he
amhail,	efel,	like
eochair,	egoriad,	a key
eidheann,	eiddew,	ivy
éidhre, frost,	eira,	snow
àireamh,	eirif,	a number
easbhuidh,	eisieu,	want
ealtuinn,	ellyn,	a razor
iomall,	emyl,	a border
anmhor,	enfawr,	huge
&c.	&c.	&c.

This might be carried on much further; but let this suffice in the meantime: it may draw the attention of more competent scholars to the subject, which is certainly not devoid of interest.

KEY

To the sounds represented by the marks used in the pronouncing columns of the following pages.

Vowels.		Gaelic standard.	Corresponding English standard.
1	ă,	fan, wait,	=făt
2	â,	nâr, shameful	=fâr
1	e,	cleas, a trick,	=beat ; or Scotch a in Kate
2	è,	fèar, a man,	=fèrvid
3	é,	céum, a step,	=a in tale, French ê in été
4	ê,	è, he	=whére
1	i,	min, meal,	=mint
2	î,	mîr, a piece	=ee in tree, or i in field
1	o,	son, sake,	=sot
2	ô,	ôr, gold,	=fôr
3	ò,	bhòs, on this side,	=bòlt
4	ō,	mōr, great,	=bōld
1	ü,	grüth, curd,	=büll, püsh
2	ū,	būth, a tent,	=trūe, rū-in
3	u,	caolus, a strait,	=us
4	û,	caol, small,	=û in French jeûne, nearly
	ў,	———	=anў

c never sounds like s; but always hard like k or q.

g never sounds like j; but always hard like q or k.

ch before or after a, o, u, in the same syllable, sounds as in the Irish word *och;* or like gh in the Scotch word *saugh,* (willow.)

ch in the same syllable with e or i, sounds as in the Scotch word fich, or as Greek χ is pronounced in Scotland.

gh in the same syllable with a, o, or u, sounds a little more obtuse than ch in the same situation.

gh in the same syllable with e, i, sounds like y in the English words ye, yield.

g. Italic g before l and n is silent. It is used to denote
a liquid sound of these letters.

*g*l sounds like liquid gl in French, (*ligne.*)

*g*n sounds like liquid gn in French, (*vigne.*)

k sounds as in king, kiss.

ll ⎫ denote a broad liquid sound of these letters, like l
nn ⎬ and n in Italian mu*l*to, *n*uovo, and r in English
rr ⎭ *r*oar.

nh are silent: they denote that the vowel preceding them
has a nasal sound.

ng denotes a sound like that of ng in the English words
hang, strong, sing, sung.

q sounds as in French que.

˘ The arch denotes a short vowel, and that the syllable
over or beneath which it is placed contains a diphthong
or triphthong.

′ The accent placed after a syllable shows that the stress
rests on the vowel or consonant preceding it.

y at the beginning of a syllable in the pronunciation co-
lumn, sounds as in ye, you.

VOCABULARY, &c.

Of the Universe.

Mu'n Chruitheachd.

English.	Gaelic.	Orthoepy.
God, *m.*	Dia,	dĭa ; dĭu, or jĭă
The Creator, *m.*	an cruthadair,	ung crüh'ud-ėr
The Godhead, *f.*	an diadhachd	un dĭu'yuchq
The Trinity, *f.*	an trianaid	un trî'ăn-ėtsh
The Father, *m.*	an t-athair,	un tah'ėr
The Son, *m.*	am mac,	um-machq'
Jesus Christ, *m.*	Iosa Criosta,	ĭu'su crîŭs-tu
The holy Spirit, *m.*	an Spiorad naomh,	un spirr'ut nûv
The creation, *m.*	{ an cruthach,	ung crüh'uch
	{ an cruthachadh,	ung crüh'uch-ugh
A creature, *m.*	créutair,	cré'tėr
The world, *m.*	an saoghal,	un sû'ull
Heaven, *m.*	neamh,	gnў̂ê'v (liq)
Hell, *f.*	ifrinn,	if rĭgn (liq)
A spirit, *m.*	spiorad.	spirr'ut
An angel, *m.*	aingeal,	ăing'gўull
The Devil, *m,*	an diabhol,	un dĭu'üll
The fairies, *m.*	na sithchean.	nu shî'chўun.

Of the Elements.

Mu na Dùilean.

The earth, *m.*	˙ an talamh,	un tal'uv
Water, *m.*	uisge,	ŭish'kўu
Fire, *m.*	teine,	tўen'u- ; tshen'u
Air, *m.*	an t-àile,	un tâ'lĭu

English.	Gaelic.	Orthoepy.
Wind, *f.*	gaoth,	gû
A storm, *f.*	stoirm,	stèr'-in ; stor'im
The North wind, *f.*	a' ghaoth tuadh,	u ghû tüä
— South — *f.*	—— deas,	u ghû dÿess
— East — *f.*	—— 'n ear,	u ghû gnÿèr (liq)
— West — *f.*	—— 'n iar,	u ghû gnîur (liq)
Thunder, *m.*	{ torunn, { tàirneanach,	torr'unn târr'gnÿèn-uch(liq)
Lightning, *m.*	dealan,	dÿal'lan
Fog, *m.*	ceò,	kÿô
A cloud, *m.*	nèul,	gnÿéll (liq)
Rain, *m.*	uisge,	uïsh'kÿu
A shower, *f.*	fras,	frass
Hail, *f.*	clach mhcallain,	klach vïèll'èn
Snow, *m.*	sneachda,	shgnïèch'qu (liq)
Frost, *m.*	reodhadh,	rèŏ'ugh ; ro'ugh
Ice, *f.*	eigh ; deigh,	eï ; dïeï
Thaw, *m.*	aiteamh.	ăiht'uv.

Of Colours.

Mu Dhaithean.

A rainbow, *m.*	bodha froise,	bŏŭ frosh'u
A colour, *m.*	dath,	dah
White, *m.*	geal,	gïal
Black, *m.*	dubh,	düh
Blue, *m.*	gorm,	gor'om
Green, *m.*	uaine,	üaïn'u
Grey, *m.*	glas,	glass
Red, *m.*	dearg,	dïar'aq
Yellow, *m.*	buidhe,	bü-i
Brown, *m.*	donn,	döünn, dónn
Purple, *m.*	purpi ; purpur,	pur'pi ; pur'pur
Scarlet, *f.*	sgàrlaid,	skâr'laït
Lightblue, *m.*	liath-ghorm,	llia'yorm
Vermilion, *m.*	corcur,	korq'ur
Hoddengray, *m.*	liath-ghlas,	llia'ylass

OF TIME.
Mu ùine.

English.	Gaelic.	Orthoepy.	
A year, *f.*	bliadhna,	blĭu'nnu	
A month, *m.*	mìos,	mí's; mĭas	
A week, *f.*	seachdain,	shĕchq'ĕn	
A day, *m.*	là; latha,	llâ; llah'u	
An hour, *f.*	uair,	ĭuĭr; ĭaĭr	
A minute, *f.*	mineid,	min'ĕĭt	
The morning, *f.*	a' mhaduinn,	u vat'i*gn*	(liq)
Noon, *m.*	meadhoin latha,	mi-ĕn llah'u	
Evening, *m.*	feasgar,	fess'cur	
Twilight(morning)	a' chamhanaich,	u chav'an-ich	
—— (evening)	*m.*an dù-thra,	un dū'hra; dū'ra	
To-day, *m.*	an diugh,	un dĭüh; jüh	
To-morrow, *m.*	am màireach,	um mânh'rў̃uch	
The day after to-morrow, *m.*	an earair,	un *gn*ў̃ĕr'ir	(liq)
Yesterday, *m.*	an dé,	un dў̃é; or jé	
Three days hence,	an eararais,	un erarish	

DAYS OF THE WEEK.
Làithean na seachdaine.

Monday, *m.*	diluain,	di-lüaĭn
Tuesday, *m.*	dimairt,	di-mârsht
Wednesday, *m.*	diciadain,	di-kĭa'duĭn
Thursday, *m.*	didaoirn,*	di-dûĭ'rn
Friday, *m.*	dihaoine,	di-hûĭn'u
Saturday, *m.*	disathurna,	di-sah'ur-nu
Sunday, *m.*	didòmhnaich,	di-dônh'-nich

DIVISIONS OF THE YEAR.
Ràithean na bliadhna.

Spring, *m.*	ant-earrach,	un tshў̃ar'ruch
Summer, *m.*	an samhradh,	un săünh'rugh
Autumn, *m.*	{ am foghar,	um fu-ur
	am fogh'radh,	um fû'rugh
Winter, *m.*	an geamhradh,	ung gў̃ĕü'rugh

* This word is sometimes corrupted into dirdaoin.

English.	Gaelic.	Orthoepy
A quarter of a year,	ràithe, *m.*	rrâ-ï
Half a year, *f.*	leth bhliadhna	glch'vlĭu-nnu (liq)
Three quarters of a year,	} trì ràitheau.	tr râĭ'un.

Other Terms and Holidays.

Ràithean agus féillean eile.

Christmas, *f.*	*nolluig,	nuoll'ik
The new year, *f.*	a' bhliadhn' ùr	u vlĭunn ūr
Martinmas, *f.*	anfhéill màrtainn,	{ un éĭgl mars'tuĭgn (liq)
March, *m.*	am màrt,	um mâ'rst
May, *m.*	am màgh,	um mâgh
June, *m.*	an céitcin,	ung kўé'tўén
The worm month,*m.*an t-inchar,		un tўüch'ur
Lammas, *f.*	an liùnasdail,	unglўūn'us·duĭl(liq)
Lent, *m.*	au carmhus,	ung car'a-us
A holiday, *m.*	latha féille,	llah'u féĭgl-u (liq)
A fast day, *m.*	latha traisg.	llah'u trashk.

Of Mankind.

Mu'n Chinne daoine.

A man, *m.*	duine,	düïn'u
A woman, *m.*	boireannach,	boĭr'unn-uch
Infancy, *f.*	leanabachd,	glўén'ub-uchq (liq)
A child, *m.*	leanabh,	glўén'uv (liq)
A boy, *m.*	giullan,	gўüll'an
A girl, *f.*	caileag,	caïl'ak
A little girl, *f.*	niag,	gni-ak (liq)
Age, *f.*	aois,	û'sh
Youth, *f.*	ðige,	ôĭk'u ; ô'kўu
A youth, *m.*	ðganach,	ô'gan-uch
A lad, *m.*	gille,	gigl'lĭu (liq)
A lass, *f.*	nìonag,	gnĭ'nak (liq)

* nocl, natal, nathalig, nal'uig, nol'uig.

English.	Gaelic.	Orthoepy.
An old fellow, *m.*	bodach,	bot'tuch
An old hag, *f.*	cailleach,	kaĭgl'uch (liq)
A husband, *m.*	fear; céile,	fĕr; ké'lu
A wife, *f.*	bean; céile,	bĕn; ké'lu
A widow, *f.*	*banntrach,	băŭnn'truch
A bachelor, *m.*	fleasgach,	fless'cuch
A maid, *f.*	†maidionn,	muĭ'dў̆unn
A father, *m.*	athair,	ah'ĕr
A mother, *f.*	màthair,	mânh'ĕr; mê'ĕr
A brother, *m.*	bràthair,	brâ'ĕr
A sister, *f.*	piuthar,	pĭŭ'ur

OF KINDRED.
Mu Luchd dàimh.

Ancestors, *m.*	sinnsreadh,	shînh'shrugh
Relations, *m.*	càirdean,	câr'dў̆un
A grandfather, *m.*	seanair,	shў̆ĕn'ĕr
A grandmother, *f.*	seanmhair,	shў̆ĕn'a-vĕr
A greatgrandfather,	sinnseanair, *m.*	shînh'shў̆ĕn-ĕr
A great grand- mother, *f.* }	sinnseanmhair,	shînh'shў̆ĕn-a-vĕr
Children,	clann (*f. sing.*),	kllăŭnn
Offspring, *m.*	sliochd,	sllў̆uchq
A son, *m.*	mac; machd,	mak; machq
A daughter, *f.*	nighean; nion,	gni-au
A grandson or granddaughter, }	odha, *m.*	ŏŭ

INDIRECT KINDRED.
Luchd cleamhnuis.

A father-in-law, *m.*	athair céile,	ah'ĕr ké'lu
A mother-in-law, *f.*	mathair chéile,	mânh'ĕr ché'lu
A son-in-law, *m.*	cliamhuinn,	klĭu'ign (liq)
A daughter-in-law,	banachliamhuinn, *f.*	ban'a chlĭu'ign (liq)

---

* Bantrach and baintreach. † *Madonna.*

English.	Gaelic.	Orthoepy.
A brother-in-law,	bràthair céile, m.	brâ'er ké'lu
A sister-in-law, f.	piuthar chéile,	piü'ur ché'lu
A foster mother, f.	muime,	müĭm'u
A foster father, m.	oide,	uĭtsh'u
A foster child, m.	dalta,	dall'tu
A nurse, f.	banaltrum,	ban'all-trum
A god-father, m.	oide,	uĭtsh'u
A god-mother, f.	muime,	müĭm'u
A god-son or daughter, m. }	dalta,	dall'tu
A sponsor, m.	goisti.	gosh'tshi ; gosht'i.

Of the Body.

Mu'n chorp.

The body, m.	an corp,	ung corp
The members,	na buill,	nu büĭgl (liq)
A member, m.	ball,	bäüll
The head, m.	an ceann,	ung kўeünn
The hair, m.	am falt,	um fallt
The face, m.	an t-aodunn,	un tû'dn
The front, f.	an aghaidh,	un ugh'i
The visage, f. {	a' ghnùis,	u ghrū'sh
	an ùrla,	un ūr'llu
The eyebrows,	na maildhean,	nu mé'lĕ-un
The eyes,	na sùilean,	nu sū'lўun
The eyelids,	na fàbhran,	nu fâ'v-run
The eyelashes,	na ruisg,	nu rüshk
The nose, f.	an t-sròn	un trô'n
The nostril, m.	an cuiunein,	ung cuĭgn'en (liq)
The cheek, f.	a' ghruaidh	u ghrüaĭ-y
The jaw, m.	am peirceal	um per'kўull (liq)
The slope of the cheek, f. }	an leachd,	un glўéchq
The chin, f.	an smig,	un smik
The mouth, m.	am béul,	um bé'll ; bĭall

English.	Gaelic.	Orthoepy.
The lips,	na bilean	nu bil'un
The teeth,	na fiaclan,	nu fĭuch'cllun
The tongue, *f.*	an teanga,	un tўĕng'gu.
The ears,	na cluasan,	nu kllüǎs'un
The neck, *f.*	an amhach,	un ăüch
The shoulder, *f.*	a' ghualainn,	u ghüŭll'iɳn (liq.)
The arm, *m.*	an gàirdein,	ung gâr'dўĕn
The elbow, *f.*	an uileann,	un üïl'unn
The hand, *f.*	an làmh,	un llânhv
The fingers,	na meòir,	nu mўôĭr
The thumb, *f.*	an òrdag,	un ô'r-daq
The first finger, *f.*	a' chorag,	u chor'aq
The little finger, *f.*	an lùdag,	un llū'daq
The fist, *m.*	an dòrn,	un dôrnn
A joint, *m.*	alt,	allt
A nail, *f.*	ionga,	iŭng'gu
The knuckles,	na rùdain,	nu rū'd-ĕn
A palm, *f.*	bas,	bass
The breast, *m.*	an t-uchd,	un tüchq
The chest, *m.*	an cliabh,	ung klĭuv
The belly, *f.*	a' bhrù,	u vrū
The thighs,	na sléisnean,	nu shɳlé'sh-nўun
The knee, *m.*	an glùn,	ung gllūn
The kneepan, *m.*	failmein,	fĕl'ĕm-ĕn
The calf, *m.*	an calpa,	ung call'a-puh
The foot, *m.*	an troidh,	un trŭih
The heel, *f.*	an t-sàil,	un tâïl
The skull, *m.*	an claigeann,	ung kllaĭk'unn
The brain, *m.*	an t-eanachuinn,	untўĕn'uch-iɳn(liq
The heart, *m.*	an cridhe,	ung cri-u
The lungs, *m.*	an sgamhan,	un sganhv'an
The liver, *m,*	an grùdhan,	ung grū'an
The kidneys,	na h-àirnean,	nu hâr'ɳnўun (liq.)
The stomach, *m.*	an goile,	ung guïl'lўu
Blood, *f.*	fuil,	füĭl
Flesh, *f.*	feòil,	fĭôïl

English.	Gaelic.	Orthoepy.
Skin, *m.*	craiceann,	kraĭch'kўunu
A bone, *m.*	cnàimh,	kraĭv ; kráĭgh
A vein, *f.*	cuisle,	cüsh'glўu (liq)
A sinew, *f.*	féith.	fć.

FACULTIES OF THE BODY.

Céud-fathan a' chuirp.

The sight, *m.*	am fradharc,	um fru'urq
Smelling, *m.*	fàileadh,	fáĭl'ugh
Hearing, *f.*	claisteachd,	kllaĭsh'tўuchq
Taste, *m.*	blas,	blass
Feeling, *m.*	mothachadh,	moh'uch-ugh
Health, *f.*	slàinte,	sllâĭn'tўu
The constitution, *f.*	a' chàilcachd,	u châĭl'uchq.
Beauty, *f.*	àille,	âigl'glўu (liq)
Ugliness, *f.*	gnàidead,	grâĭnhd'ud
The voice, *m.*	an guth,	ung güh
A smile, *m.*	foghàire.	fŏ-ghâĭr-u
A laugh, *m.*	gàire,	gâĭr-u
Weeping, *m.*	gal ; gul,	gal ; gül
Sorrow, *m.*	mulad ; bròn,	mül'at ; brô'n
A sigh, *f.*	osna ; osunn,	os'nnu ; os'unn
Sleep, *m.*	cadal ; codal,	cat'tull ; cot'tull
Pleasure, *m.*	toileachas,	toĭl'uch-us
Joy, *m.*	aoibhneas,	ûĭv'nus
Pain, *m.*	cràdh,	krâ'gh
Hunger, *m.*	acras,	ach'qrus
Thirst, *m.*	pathadh.	pah'ugh.

DISEASES OF THE BODY.

Easlaintean a' chuirp.

A disease, *f.*	easlaint,	ess'sllâĭgnt (liq)
An illness, *m.*	tinneas,	tign'us (liq)
A disorder, *f.*	éucail,	é-kail
The toothache, *m.*	an déudiogh,	un déĭt-ugh

English.	Gaelic.	Orthoepy.
A swoon, *m.*	néul,	*gné'll* (liq)
A fainting, *f.*	laigsinn, or fàillinn,	{ *llaïk'shign* (liq) *fäïgl'ign* (liq) }
An itching, *m.*	tachus,	tach'us
Deafness, *f.*	buidhre,	büïr'u
Madness, *m.*	cuthach,	qu'uch
Rheumatism, *f.*	lòini,	llô-ni
A fever, *m.*	fiabhrus,	fïu'rus, fiav'rus
A fit, *m.*	téum,	tshy̆é'm
A shivering, *f.*	grìs; crith,	grî'sh; crih'
Delirium, *f.*	bàini.	bâ'nh-ni.

Accidents, Remedies.

Tuitcamais, Leigheis.

An accident, *m.*	tuitcamas,	tüh't̃yum-us
A scratch, *f.*	sgrìob,	scrî'p
An excoriation, *m.*	rùsgadh,	rūs'qugh
A wrest, *m.*	sniomh,	sgnïäv (liq)
A sprain, *m.*	caisleachadh	{ cash'gly̆uch-ugh (liq) }
A swelling, *m.*	at,	ah't
A tumour, *m.*	màn,	mânh'n
A boil, *f.*	neasgaid,	gny̆sk'ëït, (liq)
A bruise, *m.*	bruthadh,	brü'ugh
A squeeze, *m.*	fàsgadh,	fâ's-cugh
A wound, *m.*	leòn,	gly̆ô'n (liq)
A hurt, *m.*	dochunn,	doch'unn
A burning, *m.*	losgadh,	llòs'cugh
A scar, *f.*	athailt,	ah'iglt, (liq)
A cold, *m.*	cnatan,	kranh'tan
A cough, *m.*	casad,	kas'ut
A medicine, *f.*	cungaidh,	kŭng'ï
A purge, *f.*	burgaid,	bür'ug-ëït
A plaster, *m.*	plàsd,	pllâ'st.

English.	Gaelic.	Orthoepy.

Of the Mind.
Mu'n Inntinn.

English	Gaelic	Orthoepy
The soul, *m.*	au t-anam,	un tan'um
Reason, *f.*	tuigse,	tuĭk'shu
Common sense, *f.*	toinisg,	toĭn'ishk
Understanding, *f.*	tùrsuinn,	tūrs'i*y*n (liq)
Sense, *m.*	ciall,	kỹull
Thought, *f.*	smuain,	smüăĭn
Judgment	breathnachadh,	brėn'uch-ugh
Imagination, *m.*	beachd,	bėchq
Fancy, *f.*	meanmna,	mėn'ėm-nu
Will, *f.*	toil,	toĭl
Desire, *m.*	iarrtus; togradh,	ĭurr'tus; toq'ru
Knowledge, *m.*	eòlas,	iô'llus
Memory, *f.*	meoghair,	mỹŏ'ir
Recollection, *f.*	cuimhne,	cuĭ'nu
Hope, *m.*	dòchus,	dô'chus.
Fear, *m.*	eagal,	eq'ull
Shame, *f.*	nàire,	nnânh'rỹu
Dread, *m.*	uamhas,	üănh'vass
Grief, *m.*	bròn,	brô'n
Despair, *m.*	éu-dòchas,	é-dô'chus
Terror, *f.*	oillt.	uĭ*g*l't (liq)

Virtues of the Mind.
Subhailcean na h-inntinn.

English	Gaelic	Orthoepy
Virtue, *f.*	subhailc,	süh'ailk
Charity, *m.*	oirchios,	oĭr'i-chỹus
Justice, *m.*	ceartas,	kỹars'tus
Temperance, *f.*	stuamachd,	stüăm'uchq
Modesty, *f.*	màlltachd,	mânhll'tuchq
Bashfulness, *f.*	nàrachd,	nnânh'ruchq
Politeness, *m.*	suairceas,	süŭir'kỹus
Honesty, *m.*	ionracas,	ĭünh'rru-cus
Sweetness, *m.*	grinneas,	gri*y*n'us (liq)

English.	Gaelic.	Orthoepy.
Goodness, *m.*	mathas,	mah'us
Patience, *f.*	foighidinn,	fuĭ'i-di*g*n (liq)
Prudence, *f.*	crionndachd,	criunn'duchq
Industry, *m.*	dìcheall,	dîchў̆ull
Honour, *f.*	onoir,	on'ér
Economy, *f.*	caontachd,	kû'n-tuchq
Wisdom, *m.*	gliocas,	glў̆uch'cus
Courage, *f.*	misneach,	mish'*g*nў̆uch (liq)
Innocence, *m.*	neochiontas,	*g*nў̆o'chў̆untus (liq)
Generosity, *f.*	féil, fialachd,	fé'il, fial'uchq (liq)
Boldness, *f.*	dànachd,	dânhn'uchq
Emulation, *f.*	farpais,	farp'ĕsh
Pity, *m.*	truas,	trü'ūs
Penitence, *m.*	aithreachas,	aĭr'uch-us
Hardihood, *m.*	cruadal,	crüŭ'tal
Gratitude, *f.*	taingealachd.	taĭng'gў̆al-luchq.

VICES OF THE MIND.

Dubhailcean na h-inntinn.

Vice, *f.*	dubhaile,	duh'ăilk
Avarice, *m.*	an gionach,	ung gў̆un'uch
Pride, *f.*	spòrs; pròis,	spôr's ; prô'sh
Envy, *m.*	farmad,	far'am-ut
Ignorance, *m.*	aineolas,	aĭn'ĭoll-us
Idleness, *m.*	diamhanas,	diă'van-us
Gluttony, *f.*	geòcaireachd,	gў̆ô'chq-ir-èchd
Calumny, *f.*	cùl-chainnt,	cüll'chaĭ*g*nt (liq)
Impudence, *m.*	ladarnas,	llat'tarr-nnus
Cowardice, *f.*	gealtachd,	gў̆all'tuchq
Cruelty, *f.*	cruadalas,	crüă'dall-us
Ambition, *f.*	meud-mhór,	mét-vōr'
Hatred, *m.*	fuath,	füăh
Anger, *f.*	fearg,	fér'aq
Revenge, *m.*	diùbhaltas,	dĭü'ull-tus
Theft, *f.*	mèirle,	mê'r-*g*lў̆u (liq)

English.	Gaelic.	Orthoepy.
Perfidy, *f.*	foill,	fuïgl (liq)
A lie, *f.*	bréug,	bré'q
Drunkenness, *f.*	misg,	mishk
Haughtiness, *m.*	àrdan,	âr'tan
Prodigality, *m.*	anacaitheamh,	an'a-kaïh'uv
A grudge, *m.*	diùm,	diūm

FOOD AND DRINK.

Biadh 'us Deoch.

English	Gaelic	Orthoepy
Nourishment, *f.*	beatha, or teachd-antìr,	bĕh'u tÿĉchq-un-tshîr'
A meal, *m.*	lòn bidh, longadh,	or- { llô'n bî'gh / llóng'gu
Food, *m.*	biadh,	bîûgh
Bread, *m.*	aran,	ar'an
Oatmeal cake,	aran coirce,	ar'an koïr'kÿu
Barley bread,	—— còrna,	—— ïô'r-nnu
Wheat bread,	—— cruineachd,	—— cruïn'nÿuchq
Rye bread,	—— seacail,	-—shÿŏq'cuïgl (liq)
A bit, *m.*	crioman,	krim'an
A slice, *f.*	snaois,	snnû'sh
Fish, *m.*	iasg,	îûsq
Flesh, *f.*	feòil,	fÿòï'l
Boiled meat, *f.*	feòil bhruich,	fÿô'ïl vrüïch
Roast meat, *f.*	feòil ròiste,	fÿô'ïl rrô'sh-tÿu
Venison, *f.*	sitheann,	shih'unn
An egg, *m.*	ubh,	ügh
Cheese, *m.*	càise,	kâ'shu
Beef, *f.*	mairt-fheoil,	marsht'él
Mutton, *f.*	muilt-fheoil,	müïglt'él (liq)
Lamb, *f.*	uain-fheoil,	ilaïn'él
Veal, *f.*	laoigh-fheoil,	llûïgh'él
Pork, *f.*	muic-fheoil,	müïchk'él
Goat's flesh,	gaidhr'-fheoil,	gûïr'él
Tripe, *f.*	maodal,	mûnh'dll

D

English.	Gaelic.	Orthoepy.
A blood pudding, *m.*	créathachan,	cré'uch-an
A stuffed pudding, marag, *f.*		mar'ak
Minced meat, *f.*	biadh pronn,	biŭgh próünn
A haggis, *f.*	taigeis,	taĭk'esh
Porridge,	{ lite, *f.* or { brochan, *m.*	{ *g*lih'tў̃u (liq) { broch'an
Sowins, *f.*	cà'bhrigh,	cäü'rich
Brose, *m.*	bruthaiste,	brü'ĕsh-tў̃u
Meal, *f.*	min,	mĭn
Pease, *f.*	peasair,	pess'ir
Beans, *f.*	pònair,	pô'n-ir
Wine, *m.*	fion,	fĭan, or fĭ'n
Beer, *m.*	leann,	*g*lў̃ĕünn (liq)
Black beer, *f.*	beòir,	bў̃ôĭr
Whisky, *m.*	uisge beatha,	uĭsh'kў̃u beh'u
Milk, *m.*	bainne,	baĭ*g*n'*g*nў̃u (liq)
Cream, *m.*	cè ; ciath,	kê ; kĭa
Whey, *m.*	méug,	mĕ̆ōq ; mé'q.

SEASONINGS, &c.

Blasrachd, &c.

Salt, *m.*	salunn,	sall'unn,
Spices, *m.*	spìsreadh,	spĭ'sh-rugh
Vinegar, *m.*	fion géur,	fĭ'n gў̃é'r
Oil, *f.*	ola,	oll'llu
Butter, *m.*	ìm,	î'm, or imɪn
Gravy, *m.*	sùgh,	sūgh
Sauce, *f.*	brìgh,	brî-y.

MEN'S APPAREL.

Uigheam fhirionnach.

Cloth, *m.*	aodach,	û'duch
Home made cloth, *m.*	clò,	kllô
Clothes, *f.*	uigheam,	üĭ-um
A suit, *f.*	deise,	dў̃csh'ɪɪ

English.	Gaelic.	Orthoepy.
A cap, *m.*	currachd,	cürr′uchq
A hat, *f.*	ad,	att
A coat, *m.*	còta,	côh′tu
A vest, *f.*	peiteag,	peh′tўak
Trousers, *f.*	briogais,	brĭq′ish
Drawers, *f.*	dradhais,	drah′ish
Hose,	osain,	oss′ên
Shoes,	bròg·n,	brô′q-un
A plaid, *m.*	breacan,	brêch′kan
A kilt, *m.*	feile beag,	fel′u-bcq′
A belted plaid,	breacan an fhéili′	brech′can un é-li
A belt, *m.*	crios,	kriss
A pin, *m.*	dealg,	dўall′ak
A shirt, *f.*	léine,	glé′nu (liq)
Sleeves,	muilichinnean,	müil′ich-iɣn-un(liq)
Buttons,	cnaip,	kraĭhp
A handkerchief, *f.*	neapaicin,	gné pi-kin
A watch, *f.*	uaireadair,	ūăĭr′ut-êr
Boots,	bòtainnean,	bô′h-tuɣn-ĭun (liq)
Spurs,	spuir,	spüĭr.

WOMEN'S APPAREL.

Uigheam Bhoircannach.

A petticoat, *m.*	cota bàn,	coh-tu-bân
A gown, *m.*	gùn,	gū′nhn
Corsets, *m.*	cliabhan,	clĭu′van
A ribbon, *m.*	stìm,	shtĭ′m
A knot, *m.*	dos,	doss
Tags, tassels,	babagan,	bap′a-gun
Curls,	caisreagan,	cash′ra-gun
Trinkets,	aigleanan,	aĭk′lên-un
Gloves,	làmhainnean,	llânhv′iɣn-un (liq)
A mantle, *f.*	tonnag,	tòn′aq
A matron's cap, *f.*	sùbag,	sū′p-aq

OF A HOUSE.

Mu thigh.

English.	Gaelic.	Orthoepy.
The wall, *m.*	am balla,	um ball'llu
Buildings, *f.*	treothair,	trўo'ïr
A building,*f.*	aitreamh,	aïht'riv
A beam, *f.*	sail,	saïl
The passage, *m.*	catha,	qa'uh
A post, *m.*	gobhal,	góull
A side-beam, *m.*	taobhan,	tû'v-an
Side standards,	aitnean,	aïht'nўuɡn (liq)
The roof, *f.*	an druim,	un druïm
The roof-tree,	am maide-droma,	um maïtsh'u dróm-u
The thatch, *m.*	an tuthadh,	un tüh'ugh
A door, *m.*	dorus,	dor'us
A couple-bend, *m.*	crùb,	qrūp
A window, *f.*	uinneag,	uïɡn'ɐq (liq)
A vent, *m.*	luidheir,	lluï'ér
A hearth, *m.*	teintein,	tĕɡn'tўén (liq)
The floor, *m.*	an t- rlar,	un tūr'-llar
A partition, *f.*	clàiridh,	cllâ'ri
A room, *m.*	seòmar,	shўô'm-ur
A stair, *f.*	staidhir,	staï'ir
A ladder, *m.*	fàradh,	fâ'r-rugh.

HOUSE-FURNITURE.

Earnais tighe.

A table, *m.*	bòrd,	bô'rt
A chair, *f.*	cathair,	kah'ér
A stool, *m.*	furın,	für'um
A chest, *f.*	ciste,	kish'tўu
A pot, *f.*	poit,	poïht
A pan, *f.*	aghainn,	u'iɡn (liq)
A tub, *f.*	cùdainn ; tuba,	cū't·iɡn; tüp'u (liq)
A beaker or bicker,	meadar, *m.*	mét'tur

English.	Gaelic.	Orthoepy.
A cogue or cog, *f.*	cuach ; cuman, *m.*	cū'uch ; cüm'an
A ladle, *m.*	ladar ; liadh,	llat'tur ; llîugh
A spoon, *f.*	spàin,	spâ'ĭn, or spê'n
A knife, *f.*	sgian,	skiãn
A fork, *m.*	gramaiche,	gram'ich'u
A plate, *m.*	truinnseir,	truĭnhsh'ér
A cup, *m.*	còrn ; cuach, *f.*	côrnn ; cüŭch
A bed, *f.*	leaba,	*gl*ȳêp'u (liq)
A bed-cover, *m.*	brat,	braht
A blanket, *f.*	plaide,	pllaĭt'tshu
Sheets,	plaithean lìn,	pllaĭh'un *gl*î'n (liq)
Curtains,	sgàilean,	skâĭl'un
A pair of bellows, *m.*	balg séididh,	ball'aq shê'tshi
—— of tongs, *m.*	clodha,	cllô'uh
—— of snuffers, *m.*	smàladair,	smanhll'ut-ér
An oven, *f.*	àmhuinn,	ânh'üĭ*gn* (liq)
A pail, *f.*	cuinneag,	cuĭ*gn*'aq (liq)
A lamp, *m.*	crùisgein,	crūsh'kӯen
A candle, *f.*	coinneal,	cuĭgn'nӯull (liq)
A candlestick, *m.*	coinnleir,	cuĭ'*gl*ӯér (liq)
A looking-glass, *m.*	sgàthan,	skâ'an
A skin bottle, *f.*	searrag,	shӯar'aq
A glass, *f.*	glaine,	glluĭn'u.

OF A TOWN.

Mu Bhaile.

English.	Gaelic.	Orthoepy.
A town, *m.*	baile,	baĭl'u
A city, *f.*	caithir,	cah'ir
A church, *f.*	eaglais,	eq'lluĭsh
An inn, *m.*	tigh-òsda,	tuĭ ô's-tu
A tavern, *m.*	tigh-tàirne,	tuĭ tâĭr'*gn*ӯu (liq)
A shop, *m.*	bùth,	bū'h
A house, *m.*	tigh,	tuĭh, taih
A street, *f.*	sràid ; stràid,	srâit ; strâĭt
A passage, *m.*	rathad,	rrah'ut

English.	Gaelic.	Orthoepy.
A bridge, *f.*	drochaid,	droch'it
A school-house, *m.*	tigh-sgoile,	tuïh scoïl'u
A school, *f.*	sgoil,	scoïl
A college, *f.*	àrd-sgoil,	ârt-scoïl
An infirmary, *m.*	tigh-eiridin,	tuïh eïr'it-in
A court house, *m.*	tigh-mòid,	tuïh môït
A market-house, *m.*	tigh-margaidh,	tuïh mar'ak-i
A bake-house, *m.*	tigh-fuinidh,	tuïh füïgn'i (liq)
A slaughter-house,	tigh-slachdraidh,	mtuïh sllachq'ri
A market, *m.*	margadh,	mar'ak-ugh
The corn-market,	margadh a' ghràin,	mar'ak-ugh-u-ghrâïn
The flesh — *m.*	— na feòla,	— nu fyŏ'll-u
The fish — *m.*	— an éisg,	— un é'shk
The poultry — *m.*	— nan éun,	— nun é'n
A brew-house, *m.*	tigh-togalach,	tuïh tòk'all-uch
A foundery, *f.*	fùrnais,	fü'r-nèsh
A tanyard, *f.*	lann-chairtidh,	lläünn-charst'i
A stable, *m.*	stàbul,	stâh'pull
A cart, *f.*	cairt,	karsht
A wheel, *m.*	rotha,	roh'u.

Of a Church.

Mu Eaglais.

The altar, *f.*	an altair,	un allt'ïr
The pulpit, *f.*	a' chrannag,	u chrann'ak
A bell, *m.*	clag,	kllaq
The churchyard, *m.*	an cladh,	ung kllugh
A grave, *f.*	uaigh,	üäïgh
A coffin, *f.*	ciste mhairbh,	kish'tÿu ver'iv.

Ceremonies of the Church.

Deasghnathan na h-eaglais.

A burial, *m.*	tiodhlacadh,	tÿull'u-cugh
A sermon, *f.*	searmoin,	shÿér'um-èn

English.	Gaelic.	Orthoepy.	
The text, *m.*	an teagasg,	un tỹeq'usk	
A psalm, *f.*	salm,	sal'am	
A prayer, *f.*	ùrnuigh,	ūr'ɡni	(liq)
Singing, *f.*	seinn,	sheĭɡn	(liq)
A sacrament, *f.*	sàcramaid,	sâch'cru-mĕĭt	
Baptism, *m.*	am baisteadh,	um bash'tỹugh	
Marriage, *m.*	pòsadh,	pôs-ugh	
A session, *m.*	seisein,	sheĭsh'ĕn	
A fine, *m.*	ùmhladh,	ūnh'llugh.	

OF COMMERCE AND TRADES.

Mu mharsandachd agus mu chéirdean.

English.	Gaelic.	Orthoepy.	
A merchant, *m.*	ceannaiche or marsanda,	kỹénn'ich-u mar'sn-du	
A shopkeeper, *m.*	fear-bùth,	fĕr būh	
A trade, *f.*	cèaird,	kỹâĭrt, or kêĭrt	
A printer, *m.*	clòthadair,	kllô'h-ut-ér	
A dyer, *m.*	dathadair,	dah'ut-ér	
A mason, *m.*	clachair,	kllach'ér	
A joiner, *m.*	saor,	sû'r	
A cooper, *m.*	cùbair,	cū'p-ér	
A smith, *m.*	gobha,	góh'u	
A baker, *m.*	fuineadair,	fŭĭɡn'ut-ér	(liq)
A butcher, *m.*	feòladair,	fỹô'll-ut-ér	
A tanner, *m.*	cairtear,	carsht'ér	
A shoemaker, *m.*	gréusaiche,	grĭas'ich-u; grês'ich-u	
A tailor, *m.*	tàillear,	tâĭɡl'ér	(liq)
A saddler, *m.*	diollaidear,	dỹull'ut-êr	
A weaver, *m.*	figheadair,	fih'ut-ér	
A maltster, *m.*	brachadair,	brach'ut-ér	
A gardener, *m.*	gàradair,	gâ'r-ut-ér	
A brewer, *m.*	grùdaire,	grūd'i-ru	
A fletcher, *m.*	leisdear,	ɡlỹesh'tỹér	(liq)
A turner, *m.*	tuairnear,	tñâĭr'ɡnỹér	(liq)

English.	Gaelic.	Orthoepy.
A foxhunter, *m.*	brochdear,	brochq'ẽr
A mariner, *m.*	maraiche,	mar'-ich-u.

IMPLEMENTS OF TRADE.

Buill·oibre.

A hammer, *m.*	òrd,	ô'rt
A plane, *m.*	locair,	llochq'ir
A saw, *m.*	tuireasg ; sàbh,	tüïr-usq ; sâ'v
An adze, *f.*	tàl,	tâll
An axe, *f.*	tuadh,	tūãgh
An auger, *m.*	toradh,	torr'u
A vise, *m.*	gramaiche,	gram'ich-u
A chisel, *f.*	gilb,	gil'ip
A last, *m.*	ceap,	kẽhp
An awl, *m.*	minidh,	min'i
Pincers, *f.*	durcais,	dür'cash
A needle, *f.*	snàthad,	snnânh'ut
Scissors, *m.*	siosar,	shiss'ar
Shears, *f.*	deamhais,	$\left\{\begin{array}{l}\text{dy̆ch'ish ; or}\\\text{dẽnh'ish}\end{array}\right.$
A loom, *f.*	beairt,	bẽrsht
A shuttle, *m.*	spàl,	spâ'll
A reed, *f.*	slinn,	sglî'gn (liq)
A spade, *m.*	coibe,	cuïp'u
A knife, *f.*	sgian,	skîăn
A crow-bar, *f.*	gèamhlag,	gy̆ê'nh-ly̆aq
A wedge, *m.*	geinn,	gẽĩgn (liq)
Compasses, *m.*	gobhal-ruinn,	gò'ull ruĩgn (liq)
A mall, *m.*	farachan,	far'a-chan.

RURAL AFFAIRS.

Nithean dùchail.

The country, *f.*	an dùthaich	un dū'ich
A hill, *m.*	monadh,	mon'ugh
A mountain, *f.*	béinn,	béĩgn (liq)

English.	Gaelic.	Orthoepy.
A valley, *m.*	srath ; strath,	srah ; strah
A river, *f.*	amhuinn,	ăü'ign (liq)
A bank, *f.*	bruach,	brūăch
A field, *m.*	raon ; achadh,	rrû'n ; ach'u
A flock, *f.*	tréud,	tré't
Black cattle, *m.*	crodh,	cròh
Sheep,	caoirich,	cû'rich
Goats,	gabhair,	gó'ir
A cot, *m.*	bothan,	boh'an
A fold,	crò ; *m.* mainnir,*f.*	crò ; maïng'gir
A fank, *m.*	fang,	fang'q
Wood, *f.*	coille,	cuïgl'glўu (liq)
Heath, *m.*	fraoch,	frû'ch
Grass, *m.*	féur,	fé'r ; fê'r ; fïar.

AGRICULTURE.
Tuathanas.

Peasantry, *f.*	tuath,	tüă
A farm, *f.*	gabhail,	gah'él, gav'el
A lease, *f.*	aonta,	û'n-tu
Cattle, *f.*	féudail,	fé'daïl
A horse, *m.*	each,	éch (ch as in loch)
An ox, *m.*	damh,	dav ; dăünh
A plough, *m.*	crann,	crăünn
A furrow, *f.*	clais,	clash
A yoke, *f.*	cuinng,	cŭing'k, or cŭî-y
A withe, *m.*	gad,	gatt
A chain, *f.*	slabhruidh,	sllăü'ri
A halter, *m.*	taod,	tû't
Manure, *m.*	mathach,	mah'uch
Ploughing, *m.*	treabhadh,	trўo'ugh
A harrow, *f.*	cliath,	clïa
A ditch, *f.*	stang,	stang'q
A trench, *f.*	dìg,	dï'k
Land, *m.*	fearann,	fër'unn (liq)
Ground, *m.*	talamh,	tall'uv

English.	Gaelic.	Orthoepy.
Lime, *m.*	aol,	û'll
Clay, *f.*	crè ; criadh,	crê ; crïa
Wreck,sea-weed,*f.*feamuinn,		fém'i*g*n (liq)
Cast-ware, *m.*	ròd,	rrô'tt
A dung-hill, *m.*	dùn,	dû'n
A garden, *m.*	lios,	*g*liss (liq)
A rake, *m.*	ràsdal ; ràchdan,	râ's-tull; râ'ch-can
A dibble, *f.*	pleadhag,	plêh'ak
Reaping, *f.*	buain,	büaïn
A sickle, *m.*	corran,	corr'rran
A scythe,	speal ; *f.* fal, *m.*	spy̆êl ; fâl
A sheaf, *f.*	sguab,	scŭăp
A shock, *f.*	adag,	at'ak
A hay-cock, *m.*	turadan,	türr'ut-an
A stack, *f.*	cruach,	crüăch
Grain, *m.*	siol,	shïŭll
A barn, *m.*	sabhul,	săü'-ull
Stubble, *f.*	fasbhuain,	fass'i*g*n (liq)
Chaff, *m.*	moll,	möüll
Crop, *m.*	bàrr,	bâ'rr
Straw, *m.*	fodar,	fot'tur
A straw or hayrope, siaman, *m.*		shïa'man
A flail, *m.*	buailtean,	büăïgl'ty̆en (liq)

FRUITS.
Measan.

An apple, *m*	ubhal,	ü'ull
A pear, *m.*	péur,	pé'rr
A cherry, *f.*	siris,	shir'ish
Geans, *m.*	gingis,	ging'g-ish
Plums, *m.*	plùmbais,	pllü'm-bish
A strawberry, *m.*	suth-làir,	süh-llâïr'
Gooseberries, *f.*	gròiscidean,	gró'sh-ĕ̆ĭt-un
Berries(in general)dearcan, *f.*		dy̆ark'un
A whortleberry, *f.*braoileag,		brüĭl'ak
Raspberries, *f.*	suitheagan,	suĭ'ak-un

English.	Gaelic.	Orthoepy.
Brambleberries, *f.*	sméuran,	smê'run ; smiă'run
Hips, *f.*	mucagan,	müchk'aq-un
Haws, *f.*	sgeachagan,	skўĕch'aq-un
Sloes, *f.*	àirneagan,	âr*g*nў̈ak'un (liq)
Mountain - ash berries, (rowans) *f.*	caoran,	cû'rr-un.

VEGETABLES.

Lusan.

Greens, *m.*	càl gorm,	câll gor'um
Cabbage, *m.*	càl ceairtleach,	câll kĕrsh'*g*lў̈uch (liq)
A turnip, *f.*	nèp,	*g*nў̈êhp (liq)
A carrot, *m.*	curran,	cürr'rran
Potatoes, *m.*	buntàta,	bün-tâh'tu.

WILD PLANTS.

Luibhean fiadhaich.

Nettles, *f.*	deanntag,	dў̈ĕünn'tak
Hemlock, *f.*	iteotha,	i-tў̈o'u
Dock, *f.*	copag,	cohp'ak
Sorrel, *f.*	sealbhag,	shў̈all'u-vak
Bugloss, *m.*	am bog-lus,	um bók'-lluss
Chicken-weed, *m.*	fliodh,	flíugh
Moss, *f.*	còinneach,	cō̄ĭ*g*n'uch (liq)
Fern, *m.*	raineach,	rraĭn'uch
Lichen, *m.*	cnotul,	cronh'tull.

TREES.

Craobhan.

A tree, *f.*	craobh,	cr 'v
An ash tree, *f.*	—— uinnsinn,	— uĭnh'shi*g*n (liq)
A fir tree, *f.*	—— ghiubhais,	— yïü'ish
An elm tree, *f.*	—— leamhain,	— *g*lў̈ĕv'ĕn (liq)
A willow tree, *f.*	—— sheilich,	— hel'ich
A mountain ash, *f.*	—— chaoruinn,	— chû'r-i*g*n (liq)

English.	Gaelic.	Orthoepy.
A thorn tree, *f.*	croabh, sgithich,	crû'v skih'ich
An aspen tree, *f.*	—— chrithinn,	— chrih'ign (liq
A yew tree, *f.*	—— iubhair,	— ïü'ir
A vine tree, *m.*	fionan,	fî'n-an ; fîan'an
The bark, *f.*	cairt,	carsht
A branch, *f.*	géug,	gy̆é'q, gy̆aq
The root, *m.*	am bun,	um bühn
The top, *m.*	am bàrr,	um bâ'rr
The root, *m.*	am frèumh,	um frênhv
A fibre, *f.*	freumhag,	frê-vag
A spray, *m.*	meangan,	meng'gan.

VEGETATION.
Fàs.

The sap, *m.*	an snothach,	{ un snnonh'uch, or sno'uch
Blossom, *m.*	blàth,	bllâh
A leaf, *f.*	duilleag,	düĭgl'ak (liq)
Foliage, *m.*	duilleach,	duĭgl'ĭuch (liq)
A shoot, *m.*	meangan,	meng'gan
A twig, *f.*	bunnsag,	bünh'sak
A sapling, *m.*	ògan,	ô'can
The pith, *m.*	an glaodhan,	ung gllû'gh-an
Rosin, *f.*	bìdh	bî
The seed, *f.*	an fhras,	un rass
The kernel, *f.*	an éitne,	un ê'ht-ny̆u
A bud, *f.*	gucag,	güch'cak.

METALS.
Meatailtean.

Gold, *m.*	òr,	ô'rr
Silver, *m.*	airget ; airgiod	ėr'ĕk-ut
Iron, *m.*	iarunn,	ïŭrr'unn
Pewter, *m.*	feòdar ; fleòdar	fy̆ô'tur ; fly̆ô'tur
Lead, *f.*	luaidhe,	llüñ'ĭ
Tin, *f.*	stàin,	stâïnhn.

Astronomy.

Réul-eolas.

English.	Gaelic.	Orthoepy.
The sky, *f.*	an spéur,	un spé'rr
The east, *f.*	an àird an ear,	un *gn*y̆e̊r (liq)
The west, *f.*	—— an iar,	un *gn*y̆ar (liq)
The north, *f.*	an àirde tuadh,	un âĭr'ty̆u tü̆ă̆
The south, *f.*	an àirde deas,	un âĭr'ty̆u dy̆ess
A star, *f.*	runnag ; réul	rrünn'ak ; rré'll
The sun, *f.*	a' ghrian,	u ghrîăn
The moon, *f.*	a' ghealach,	u y̆iall'uch
The pleiades, *m.*	an grioglachan,	ung griq'lluch-an
Charles's wain, *m.*	an crann,	ung crăünn
The aurora borealis,	na fir-chlis,	na fir-chlish'
An eclipse, *m.*	duabhar,	dü̆ă̆'ur
A meteor, *f.*	caoir,	cûĭr.

Geography.

Cruinneolas.

The globe, *m.*	an cruinne,	ung cruĭ*gn*'u (liq)
A continent, *m.*	tir mòr,	tshir-mōr
Asia, *f.*	an Aisi,	un â'shi
Africa, *f.*	an Afric,	un â'frik
America, *m.*	America,	a-mer'i-cah
Europe, *f.*	an roinn còrpa,	un ruĭ*gn* ĭôr'pu
An empire, *f.*	ìmpireachd,	î'm-pir-uchk
A kingdom, *f.*	rìgheachd,	rrî'uchk.

Of Music.

Mu Cheòl.

Music, *m.*	ceòl,	ky̆ô'll
Melody, *m.*	binneas,	bi*gn*'us (liq)
A tune, *m.*	port,	porst
An air or melody,	fonn ; *m.* séis, *f.*	föünn ; shé'sh
A song, *m.*	òran,	ô'ran
A note, *m.*	póng,	pöüng

E

English.	Gaelic.	Orthoepy.
Tune, tempera-ment,	gléus, *m.*	glé'ss
A shake, *m.*	gearradh,	gȳarr'ugh
Taste, *m.*	blas,	bllass
Execution, *f.*	fileantachd,	fil'ann-tuchq
A performer, *m.*	fear-ciùil,	fĕr kȳūïl.

MUSICAL INSTRUMENTS.

Abhaidhean-Ciùil.

A harp, *f.*	clàrsach,	cllâ'r-such
A pipe, *f.*	pìob,	pî'p
A bagpipe, *f.*	piob mhòr,	pip-vōr'
The chanter, *m.*	am feadan,	um fet'tan
The reed, *f.*	an rifeid,	rrif'ĕït
The large drone, *m*	an dos mòr,	un doss mōr
The less drones, *m.*	na duis bheaga,	nu düsh vec'cu
A drone-reed, *m.*	goth,	goh
The mouth-piece,	an gaothaire, *m.*	ung gû'h-ir-u
The valve, *m.*	an siunnach,	un shïünn'uch
The bag, *m.*	am màla,	um mânh'lu
A violin, *f.*	fidheall,	fi'ull
A string, *f.*	téud,	tshé't
A peg, *m.*	cnagan,	crak'an
A jews-harp, *f.*	tromb,	tröüm
A flageolet, *f.*	fìdeag,	fî'tȳak
A whistle, *f.*	feadag,	fet'tak.

OF THE EARTH.

Mu'n Talamh.

An island,	eilein; *m.* ī, *f.*	eïl'én; î
A promontory,	rugha, *m.*	rrü'u
A cape. *f.*	maol,	mû'll
An isthmus, *m.*	tairbeart,	tĕr'up-arst
A desert, *f.*	fàsach,	fâ's-uch
A rock (on land) *f.*	creag,	kreq
A rock (in the sea)	sgeir, *f.*	skeïr

English.	Gaelic.	Orthoepy.
A road, *m.*	rathad,	rrah'ut
A path, *m.*	casan,	cass'an.

Of the Water.

Mu'n uisge.

The ocean, *m.*	an cuan,	ung cŭăn
The sea, *f.*	a'mhuir,	u vŭĭr
An arm of the sea,	loch, *m.*	lloch
A bay, *m.*	camus ; òban,	kam'us ; ô'p-an
A creek, *m.*	sàilean,	sâïl-èn
The tide, *m.*	{ an seòl mara,	{ un shv̆ô'll mar'u
	{ an sruth,	{ un srüh
A lake, *m.*	loch uisge,	lloch uĭsh'kў̆u
A current, *m.*	sruth,	srüh
A brook, *m.*	allt,	ă̆üllt
A pond, *m.*	lochan,	lloch'an
A fountain, *f.*	mathair-uisge,	mânh'èr ŭish'kў̆u
A marsh, *f.*	boglach,	bòk'lluch
A quagmire, *f.*	suil-chritheach,	sūïl chrih'uch
A spring, *m.*	fuaran,	füă̆r'an.

Of the Fire.

Mu'n teine.

A kindling, *m.*	fadadh,	fatt'agh
Flame, *f.*	lasair,	llass'ir
Smoke, *f.*	smùid,	smŭĭtsh
A blaze, *m.*	dreòs,	drў̆ô'ss
A spark, *f.*	srad,	sratt
Heat, *m.*	teas,	tў̆ess
A burning coal, *f.*	éubhal,	é'ull
A brand, *f.*	àithinn,	â'iɲn (liɲ)
Firewood, *m.*	connadh,	conn'ugh
Coals, *m.*	gual,	gūŭll
Peats, *f.*	mòine,	môĭn'u
Wood, *m.*	fiodh,	figh, (gh broad)
A fire, *m.*	gealbhan,	gў̆all'a-van

English.	Gaelic.	Orthoepy.
Soot, *f.*	suidh,	suĭ
Ashes, *f.*	luatha,	llüŭ´u

WILD ANIMALS.
Beathaichean fiata.

A lion, *m.*	leòmhan,	ɡlў̄o´un	(liq)
A bear, *m.*	mathan,	manh´un	
A wolf, *m.*	madadh alluidh,	mat´ugh all´i	
A wild boar, *m.*	torc nimhe,	tork ɡnih´u	(liq)
A fox, *m.*	sionnach,	shĭünn´uch	
A weasel, *f.*	neas,	ɡniss	(liq)
A badger, *m.*	brochd,	brochq	
A deer, *m.*	fiadh,	fiŭgh	
A stag, *m.*	damh,	dav, or dăü	
A hind, *f.*	eilid,	eil´itsh	
A roe, *f.*	earba,	ĕr´up-u	
A hare, *f.*	gèarr,	gў̂err	
A squirrel, *f.*	feòrag,	fў̂o´r-ak.	

TAME ANIMALS.
Beathaichean Callda.

A horse, *m.*	each,	ĕch
A foal, *m.*	searrach,	shў̆err´uch
A cow,	bó; *f.* mart, *m.*	bō ; marst
A calf, *m.*	laogh,	llû´gh
A bull, *m.*	tarbh,	,tar´av, or tar´ü
An ox, *m.*	damh,	dav, or dăü
A dog, *m.*	cù,	cū
A sheep, *f.*	caora,	cû´ru
A lamb, *f.*	uan,	ŭăn.

WILD BIRDS.
Eoin fhiadhaich.

An eagle, *f.*	iolair; fìrein, *m.*	ĭull´ir; fì´rў̆en
A hawk, *f.*	{ seobhag, { speirag,	{ shў̄oh´uk { sper´ak

English.	Gaelic.	Orthoepy.
A glede, *m.*	clamhan,	kllav'an; kllam'an
A partridge, *f.*	péurtag,	péurs'tak
A plover, *f.*	feadag,	fet'tak
A moor hen, *f.*	cearc fhraoich,	kỹark rrûĭch
A black cock, *m.*	coileach dubh,	cuĭl'uch düh
A wild duck, *f.*	lach,	llach
A solan goose, *m.*	sùlaire,	sū'll-ir·u
A gull, *f.*	faoilean,	fûĭl'unn
A tern, *m.*	stearnain,	stỹê'rr-gnỹén (liq)
A swan, *f.*	cala,	èll'u
A cuckoo, *f.*	cuäg; cuach,	cü-aq; cüŭch
A thrush, *f.*	smeòrach,	smỹô'ruch
A black-bird, *m.*	lon dubh,	llon düh
A lark, *f.*	uiseag,	üsh'ak.

TAME BIRDS.
Eoin shoirbh.

A cock, *m.*	coileach,	cuĭl'uch
A hen, *f.*	cearc,	kỹark
A chicken, *f.*	eireag,	eĭr'ak
A goose, *m.*	geadh; giadh,	gỹê'gh; gîagh
A gander, *m.*	gànradh,	gânh'rra
A gosling, *m.*	isean,	ish'én
A duck, *f.*	tunnag,	tünn'ak
A pigeon, *m.*	calman	call'a-man.

SEA FISHES.
Iasg Sàile.

A whale, *f.*	muc mhara,	müchk var'u
A pelloch, por-pus, *m.*	canach,	can'uch
A cod, *m.*	trosg,	trosq
A ling, *f.*	langa,	llang'gu
A gurnet, *m.*	cnòdan,	crônh'tan
A skate, or thorn-back, *m.*	sòrn,	sô'rnn
A flounder, *f.*	leòbag,	glỹô'b-ak (liq)

English.	Gaelic.	Orthoepy.	
A haddock, *f.*	adag,	at'ak	
A lithe, *f.*	liùbh,	glȳū,	(liq)
A dog-fish, *f.*	gobag,	góp'ak	
A herring, *m.*	sgadan,	scat'tan	
A seath, *f.*	cudain,	cüt'ign,	(liq)

SHELL FISH.
Maorach.

An oyster, *f.*	eisir,	esh'ir	
A lobster, *m.*	giumach,	gȳüm' uch	
A mussel, *m.*	fiasgan,	fiãs'can	
A periwinkle, *f.*	faochag,	fû'ch-ak	
A cockle, *f.*	coilleag,	cuǐgl' glȳak	(liq)
A lampit, *m.*	bàirneach,	bâïr'gnȳuch	(liq)
Spout-fish, *m.*	mùsgain,	mū'sk-èn	
Razor-fish, *m.*	muïrsginn,	mürs'kign,	(liq)

FRESH WATER FISHES.
Iasg uisge.

A trout, *m.*	breachd ; breac,	brèchq	
A pike, *m.*	geadas,	gȳet'tus	
A par, *m.*	bricein,	brich'kèn	
An eel, *f.*	easgunn,	ess'cunn	(liq)
A salmon, *m.*	bradan,	brat'tan	
A grilse, *f.*	bànag,	bânhn'ak.	

REPTILES.
Biasdan snàgach.

A serpent, *f.*	nathair,	nnanh'ir	
A toad, *f.*	maol mhàgain,	mû'll vânhq'èn	
A frog,	{ crâigean, *m.* { losgann, *f.*	{ krâ'kȳén { llôf'qunn	
A leech, *f.*	deala,	dȳall'u	
A snail, *f.*	seilcheag,	shel'ich-ak	
A caterpillar,	{ burus, *m.* { buruis *f.* { bratag, *f.*	{ bürr'us { bür'ish { brah'taq	

English.	Gaelic.	Orthoepy.	
An earth-worm,	biadhuinn,	bĭu'ign	(liq)
A slug, *m.*	lugus,	llük'us.	

Insects.

Péisteagan.

A moth, *f.*	leòmunn,	*g*lyō'm-unn	
A louse, *f.*	miol,	mĭăll	
A flea, *f.*	deargann,	dy̆ar'uq-unn	(liq)
A spider, *m.*	damhan-alluidh,	danhv'an all'i	
A grasshopper, *m.*	fionnan-feòir,	fy̆ū*g*n-an fy̆ô'ĭr	
A fly, *f.*	cuileag,	cüil'aq	
A butterfly, *m.*	dearabadan dé,	dy̆ar'a-bu-dan jé	
A bee, *m.*	seillein,	shy̆e*g*l'ĭén	(liq)
A wasp, *f.*	speach,	spéch (ch broad).	

Northern States of Europe.

Dùchannan tuath na h-Eòrpa.

Russia, *f.*	Ruisia,	rüsh'shi-a	
Sweden, *f.*	an t-Suain,	un tüăin	
Denmark, *f.*	Lochluinn,	lloch'llŭi*g*n	(liq)
Prussia, *f.*	Pruisia,	prüsh'-shi-a	
Holland, *f.*	an Olaind,	un ô'll-aĭnt	
England, *f.*	Sasgunn, Sasunn,	sass'unn	
Scotland, *f.*	Albuinn,	all'up-i*g*n	(liq)
Ireland, *f.*	Eirinn,	é'ĭr-i*g*n	(liq)

Southern States of Europe.

Dùchannan dcas na h-Eòrpa.

France, *f.*	an Fhraing,	un rrăingk	
Germany, *f.*	a' Ghearmailt,	u yĭér'am é*g*lt	(liq)
Turkey, *f.*	an Tuirc,	un tüĭrk	
Italy, *f.*	an Eadailt,	un ett'ăillt	
Spain, *f.*	an Spàinnt,	un spăĭ*g*n'tt	
Greece, *f.*	a' Ghréig,	u ghré'k.	

TOWNS IN EUROPE.

Bailtean 's an roinn Eòrpa.

English.	Gaelic.	Orthoepy.	
London, *m.*	Lunnuinn,	lunn'ï*g*n	(liq)
Edinburgh, *m.*	Dun-éidionn,	dün-étsh'un	(liq)
Dublin, *m.*	Bail o Cliar,	bail-o-clïŭr*	
Rome, *f.*	an Ròimh,	un rônh'i.	

NATIONAL NAMES.

Ainmean Tìreil.

A European, *m.*	†Eòrpach,	ïôr'puch	
A Russian, *m.*	Ruiseanach,	rrüsh'ĕn-uch	
A Swede, *m.*	Suaineach,	süăin'uch	
A Dane, *m.*	Lochluinneach,	lloch'lluïnn-uch	
An Englishman,*m.*	Sasunnach,	sass'unn-uch	
A Scotchman, *m.*	Albannach,	all'up-unn-uch	
An Irishman, *m.*	Earunnuch,	érr'-unn-uch	
A Dutchman, *m.*	Dùitseach,	dūït'shў̈uch	
A German, *m.*	Gearmailteach,	{ gў̈ar'am-è*g*l-tў̈uch (liq)	
A Frenchman, *m.*	Frangach,	frang'guch	
A Spaniard, *m.*	Spàinnteach,	spàïgn'ẗў̈uch	(liq)
An Italian, *m.*	Edailteach,	ett'aïg̈l'ẗў̈uch	(liq)
A Greek, *m.*	Gréugach,	gré'q-uch	
A Turk, *m.*	Turcach,	türk'uch	
A Jew, *m.*	Iùdhach,	ïū'uch	
An Egyptian, *m.*	Eiphideach,	é'fit-uch	
An American, *m.*	Americanach,	a-mer'i-can-uch	
An Indian, *m.*	Innseanach,	ính'-shў̈ĕn-uch.	

---

* Or Bail ath cliath.

† The feminine of these names is formed by prefixing the word ban (female) to each of them; thus, ban-Eòrpach, a female European, &c.

Hereditary Titles.

Ainmean oighreil.

English.	Gaelic.	Orthoepy.
A king, *m.*	rìgh; rìogh,	rrî
An emperor, *m.*	ìmpire,	îm'-pir-u
A prince, *m.*	priunnsa,	prĭūnh-su
A duke, *m.*	diùc,	dĭūchq
A marquis, *m.*	marcus,	mar'-cuss
An earl, *m.*	iarla,	îŭr'llu
A knight, *m.*	ridire,	rritsh'ir-u
A baron, *m.*	baran,	bar'-an.

Miscellaneous Titles.

Ainmean éugsamhuil.

The pope, *m.*	am pàpa,	um pâh'pu
An archbishop, *m.*	àrd easbuig,	ârt ess'pik
A bishop, *m.*	easbuig,	ess'pik
A priest, *m.*	sagart,	saq'urst
A preacher, *m.*	scarmoiniche,	shȳar'am-ĕn-ich-u
A catechist, *m.*	ceistear,	kȳesht'ĕr
A judge, *m.*	breitheamh,	brch'uv
A writer, *m.*	sgrìbheadair,	scrî'ut-ĕr
A notary, *m.*	nòtair,	nônh'tĕr
A sheriff, *m.*	siorram,	shĭurr'am
A messenger, *m.*	maor,	mû'r
A bailie, *m.*	bàillidh,	bâgli (liq)

Of Measures.

Mu Thomhaisean.

An inch, *f.*	ðirleach,	ôr'glȳuch (liq)
A span, *f.*	réis,	rré'sh
A foot, *m.*	troidh,	truĭ
A yard, *f.*	slat,	sllaht
A mile, *m.*	mìle,	mí'lu
A quarter of a yard,	càrt, *m.*	cârst
A fathom, *m.*	aitheamh,	aĭnh'uv

OF WEIGHTS.

Mu chothroman.

English.	Gaelic.	Orthoepy.
An ounce, *m.*	ùnnsa,	ūnh′su
A quarter, *m.*	cairteal,	karsh′tshўall
A pound, *m.*	pùnnd,	pū′nt
A stone, *f.*	clach,	klach
A ton, *m.*	tunna,	tünn′u.

LIQUID MEASURES.

Cuimseirean dibhe.

A glass, *f.*	gloine,	gluĭn′u
A gill, *m.*	siola,	shўul′lu
A mutchkin, *m.*	bodoch,	bot′uch
A pint, *m.*	pinnt,	pî′nt
A chopin, *m.*	seipein,	shehp′én
A gallon, *m.*	galan,	gal′lan
A cask, *m.*	buideal,	büĭt′yall
A barrel, *m.*	tunna,	tünn′u
A hogshead, *f.*	togsaid,	tòqs′étsh.

OF COINS.

Mu chùinncadh.

A farthing, *f.*	feòrling,	fўôr-*g*ling (liq)
A halfpenny, *m.*	bonn a sè	{ böünn-u shê, or shĭa
A penny, *f.*	sgilling,	ski*g*l′i*g*n (liq)
Sixpence, *f,*	sè sgilling,	sê ski*g*l′i*g*n (liq)
A shilling, *m.*	{ tastan, sgilling shasunn- ach,	{ tass′tan, ski*g*l′i*g*n has′unn- uch, (liq)
A crown, *m.*	crùn,	crū′n
A half-crown, *m.*	leth chrun,	*g*lech′rün (liq)
A guinea, *m.*	gini,	gin′ĭ
A half guinea, *m.*	leth ghini,	*g*leh yin′ĭ
A pound, *m.*	punnd sasunnach,	pūnnt sass′unn-uch

Of Names of Men.

Mu ainmean fhirionnach.

English.	Gaelic.	Orthoepy.
Allan,	Ailein,	aïl'én
Alexander,	Alastair,	all'us-tir
Andrew,	Anndra,	ăūnn'dra
Angus,	Aonghas,	un'u-us
Archibald,	Gilleasbuig,	gigl-ess'pik (liq)
Arthur,	Art,	arst
Charles,	Tèarlach,	tỹâr'lluch
Colin,	Cailein,	caïl'én
Donald,	Dònull,	dônh-null
Ewen,	Eóbhan,	ïō'un
Francis,	Frangan,	frang can
George,	Deòrsa ; Seòrus,	dỹôr'su ; shỹô'rus
Gilbert,	Gileabart,	gil'u-barst
Hector,	Eachunn,	éch'unn (ch broad)
Henry,	Eanruig,	ênh'rrik
Hugh,	Uistein,	ūsh'tshén
James,	Séumas,	shé'mus
John,	Iain, E in,	i-én ; ïôïn
Kenneth,	Coinneach,	cuïgn'yuch (liq)
Louis,	Ludhais,	llü'ésh
Malcom,	Callum,	call'um
Martin,	Màrtuinn,	mârs'tign (liq)
Michael,	Mìcheil,	mí'chél
Murdoch,	Murchadh,	mür'uch-u
Neil,	Nial,	gnîall (liq)
Norman,	Tormaid,	tor'om-étsh
Paul,	Pàl, Pòl,	pâll, pôl
Robert,	Rob,	rop
Samuel,	Somhairle,	sonh'ur-glỹu (liq)
Thomas,	Tómas,	tō'mass.

Names of Women.

Ainmean Bhoireannach.

Anna,	Anna,	ann'u

English.	Gaelic.	Orthoepy.
Beatrice,	Beatarais,	beh'turr-esh
Christian,	Cairistìona,	car'ish-tĭăn-u
Elizabeth,	Ealasaid,	ĕll'us-ĕtsh
Euphemia,	Aoirig,	ûi'rik
Grissel,	Gaorsal,	gur'sall
Helen,	Eilidh,	el'i
Jane,	Sìne,	shĭ'nu
Janet,	Seònaid,	shўô'n-ĕtsh
Isabella,	Iseabal,	ish'u-ball
Katherine,	Catrìona,	ka-trĭăn-u
Lucy,	Liùsi,	lўū'-i
Margaret,	Mairireid,	mer'ir-ĕtsh
Mary,	Màiri,	mânh'ri ; mê'ri
Rachel,	Raodhailt,	rû'iglt (liq)
Rebecca,	Beathag,	beh'ak
Sybilla,	Sibili,	ship'i-li
Susan,	Siùsaidh,	shўū'si.

NUMBER.

Aireamh.

			Literal Translation.
1 a h-aon,	u hû'n	a 1	
2 a dha,	u ghâ	a 2 (integrally)	
3 a tri,	u trî	a 3 ,,	
4 a ceithir,	u keh'ir	a 4 ,,	
5 a cóig,	u cōik	a 5 ,,	
6 a sè, or sia,	u shê, or shĭa	a 6 ,,	
7 a seachd,	u shechq	a 7 ,,	
8 a h-ochd,	u hochq	an 8 ,,	
9 a naoidh,	u nuĭ	a 9 ,,	
10 a deich,	u dўech	a 10 ,,	
11 a h-aon déug,	u hû'n dўé'q	an 11 ,,	
12 a dha dhéug,	u ghâ yĭé'q	a 2 and 10 ,,	
13 a tri déug,	u trî dўé'q	a 3 and 10 ,,	
14 a ceithir déug,	u keh'ir dўé'q	a 4 and 10 ,,	

	Orth.	Lit. tran.
15 a cóig déug,	u cōïk dy̆é′q	a 5 and 10 ,,
16 a sè, or sia déug,	u shē, or shïa dy̆é′q	a 6 and 10 ,,
17 a seachd déug,	u shèchq dy̆é′q	a 7 and 10 ,,
18 a h-ochd déug,	u hochq dy̆é′q	an 8 and 10 ,,
19 a naoidh déug,	u nuï dy̆é′q	a 9 and 10 ,,
20 à fichead,	u fich′ut	a 20 ,,
21 a h-aon thar fhichead,	u hûn har ich′ut	a 1 over 20 ,,
22 a dha, &c.	u gha, &c.	a 2 &c. ,,
30 a deich, &c.	u dy̆ech, &c.	a 10 over, &c.
31 a h-aon déug,&c.	u hû′n dy̆é′q, &c.	an 11 over 20,&c.
40 da fhich-ead,	dâ ich′ut	2 twenties
60 tri fhich-ead, &c.		3 &c.
100 céud,	ky̆é′t, or kïŭt	a 100
200 da chéud,	dâ chy̆ét	2 hundreds
300 tri, &c.		3 &c.
1000 mìle,	mî′lu	a 1000
2000 da mhìle,	da vî′lu	2 thousands
3000 tri, &c.		3 &c.
1000000 muillcin,	müɡl-ïèn (liq)	a million
da mhuillein,	dâ vüɡl′ïèn (liq)	2 millions
tri, &c.		3 &c

No higher denomination than million is used.

ORDINAL NUMBERS.

		Orth.
The 1st	an céud,	ung ky̆é′t
,, 2d	an dara,	un dar′u
,, 3d	an treas,	un tress
,, 4th	an ceathramh,	ung ky̆èr′uv
,, 5th	an cóigeamh,	ung cōïk′uv
,, 6th	an sèathamh,	un shê′uv, or shïa′uv
,, 7th	an seachdamh,	un shèchq′uv
,, 8th	an t-ochdamh,	un tochq′uv

F

Orth.

The 9th an naoidheamh,   un nuï'uv
„ 10th an deicheamh,   un dÿech'uv
„ 11th an t-aon fhear déug,   un tû'n ĕr dÿé'q
„ 12th an dara fear deug,   un dar'u fĕr dÿé'q
„ 13th an treas, fear, &c.   un tress fĕr dÿé'q, &c.

20th { am ficheadamh, *m.* um fich'ut-uv
{ an fhicheadamh, *f.* un ich'-ut-uv

21st, an céud fhear* thar fhichead—ung kÿé't ĕr har
ich'ut—the 1st one over 20 ; a' cheud té† thar
fhichead—u chyé't tshé har ich'ut.

22d, an dara fear,   } thar fhichead   un dara fĕr har ich'ut
an dara té,   ——— tshé, &c.
23d, an treas fear,   un tress fĕr, &c.
an treas té, &c.   ——— tshé, &c.

31, an t-aon fhear déug   } thar fhichead   an tû'n ĕr dÿé'q, &c.
an t-aon té déug   ——— tshé dïé'q, &c.
32, an dara fear déug   un dar'u fĕr dÿé'q, &c.
an dara té déug   ——— tshé dïé'q, &c.
33, an treas fear déug   un tress fĕr d éq, &c.
an treas té déug   ——— tshé dÿé'q
&c.   ÿ &c.

40th, an da fhicheadamh,   un da ich'ut-uv
60th, an tri ficheadamh,   un trî fich'ut-uv
80th, an ceithir, &c.   un keh'ir &c.
100th, an cóig, &c.   ung cõïk &c.
100th, an céudamh,   ung kÿé't-uv
200th, an da chéudamh,   un dà chÿé't-uv
300th, an treas céudamh, &c.   un tress kÿé't-uv
1000th, am mìle,   um mí'l·u
2000th, an dara mìle   un dar'u mí'l-u
3000th, an treas mìle, &c.   un tress mí'l·u.

---

* Fear, one; *mas.*   † té, one ; *fem.*

Adverbial Numbers.

			In the
1ly.	's a chéud àite,	su chȳé't â'tshu	1st place
2dly.	's an dara h-àite,	sun dar'u hâ'tshu	2d
3dly.	's an treas àite,	sun tress â'tshu	3d
4thly.	's a cheathramh àite,	su chȳér'uv â'tshu	4th
5thly.	's &c.		5th, &c.

Multiplicative Numbers.

once,	aon uair,	ûn üäïr,	one time
twice,	da uair,	dâ üäïr,	two times
thrice,	tri uairean,	trî üäïr'un,	three, &c
four times,	ceithir uairean,	keh'ir üäïr'un,	four, &c.
five, &c.	cóig, &c.	cōïk, &c.	five, &c.

Personal Pronouns.

Simple.

Sing.	Orth.	Plur.	Orth.
I—mi,	mì,	we,—sinn,	shîᵹn (liq)
thou,—tu, thu,	tū, ū,	you,—sibh,	shì'v
he,—e, ᴖ	ê,	} they,—iad,	iät, or êt
she,—i,	î,		

Emphatic.

Sing.		Plur.	
I—mise,	mish'u,	we,—sinne,	shiᵹn'u(liq)
thou,—tusa, thusa,	tüs'u, üs'u,	you,—sibhse,	shì'shu
he,—esan,	ess'un,	} they,—iadsan,	iät'sun
she,—ise,	ish'u,		

Compound.

I myself,—mi-féin,	mise féin,
„ tu, thu-féin,	thusa féin
„ e-féin,	esan féin
„ i-féin,	ise féin.

☞ These pronouns are all of the com. gender.

POSSESSIVE PRONOUNS.

Sing. and Plur.		Orthoepy.
my,	mo, m',	muh
thy,	do, d',	duh
his, its,	ä,	uh
her, its,	a,	uh
our,	ar,	er, and ar
your,	'ur, bhur,	er, and ür, vür
their,	än, äm,	un, um.

RELATIVE PRONOUNS.

Sing. and Plur.		Orthoepy.
who,	a,	u
which, that,	an, am,	un, um
what,	na',	nuh.

INTERROGATIVE PRONOUNS.

who?	có,	cō
what?	ciod, créud,	cutt, cré'tt
what?	'dé,	dўé, jé
which, *m.*	co è,	cò-ê
which, *f.*	co i,	cò-î.

THE NEUTER VERB *BI*. TO BE.

The root of a Gaelic verb is the 2d pers. sing. imper.

IMPERATIVE MOOD.

PRES. TENSE.

Pers.		Orthoepy.	
2. sing.	{ bi,	bí,	be
	{ bi thusa,	bí üs'u,	be thou
3d	bitheadh, e,	bi'ugh ê,	let him be
	——— i,	——— î,	let her be
1st plur.	bitheamaid,	bĭu'mit,	let us be
2d	bithibh,	bi-iv,	be you
3d	bitheadh iad,	bi-ugh ĭăt,	let them be.

INDICATIVE MOOD.

PRESENT TENSE (affirmatively).

Singular.				Plural.		
1,	2,	3,		1,	2,	3.
mi,	thu,	e,	i,	sinn,	sibh,	iad

verb *Tha,   I am.

orthoepy, hâ.

PRESENT TENSE (interrogatively).

Singular.				Plural.		
1,	2,	3,		1,	2,	3.
mi,	thu,	e,	i,	sinn,	sibh,	iad

verb, am Beil?   Am I?

orth. um bel'.

PRESENT TENSE (negatively).

Singular.				Plural.		
mi,	thu,	e,	i.	sinn,	sibh,	iad

verb, cha-n Eil,   I am not.

orth. chan ĭel'.

PAST TENSE (affirmatively).

Singular.				Plural.		
mi,	thu,	e,	i.	sinn,	sibh,	iad

verb, Bha,   I was, I have been.

orth. vâ.

PAST TENSE (interrogatively).

Singular.				Plural.		
mi,	thu,	e,	i.	sinn,	sibh,	iad

verb, an Robh?   Was I? have I been?

orth. un ròh'.

PAST TENSE (negatively).

Singular.				Plural.		
mi,	thu,	e,	i.	sinn,	sibh,	iad

verb, cha Robh,   I was not, I have not been.

orth. cha ròh'.

---

* Tha is repeated before each of the personal pronouns; so is Beil, Eil, Robh, &c.

FUTURE TENSE (affirmatively).

Singular.				Plural.		
mi,	thu,	e,	i.	sinn,	sibh,	iad

verb, Bithidh,   I shall or will be

orth. bi-iy.

FUTURE TENSE (interrogatively).

Singular.				Plural.		
mi,	thu,	e,	i.	sinn,	sibh,	iad

verb, am Bi?   Shall or will I be?

orth. um bi.

FUTURE TENSE (negatively).

Singular.				Plural.		
mi,	thu,	e,	i.	sinn,	sibh,	iad

verb, cha Bhi,   I shall or will not be.

orth. cha vî.

SUBJUNCTIVE MOOD.*

PAST TENSE (affirmatively).

                   Orthoepy.

Sing. 1. Bhithinn,   vi-ign,   I could or would be

      2. Bhitheadh tu,   vi-u tū,

      3. Bhitheadh e,   vi-ugh ê,

       ——— i,   ———î

Plur. 1. { Bhitheadh sinn, vi-u shign,

         { Bhitheadhmaid, vi-u-mîtsh,

      2. Bhitheadh sibh,   vi-u-shîv,

      3. Bhitheadh iad,   vi-ugh îăt.

---

* This tense admits of various conjunctions before it, which ma-
terially affect its signification ; thus,

na'm bithinn,	If I were, If I had been, &c.
ged bhithinn,	Though I were, though I should be, &c.
nach bithinn,	That I would or could not be.
gu'm bithinn,	That I would be, that I were.
mur bithinn,	Were I not, had I not been.
&c. &c.	&c.

PAST TENSE (interrogatively).

Orthoepy.

Sing. 1. am Bithinn,   um bi-*ign*,Could or would I be?
      2. am Bitheadh tu,   um bi-u tū,
      3. am bitheadh e,   um bi-ugh ê,
      ———— i   ——— î

Plur. 1. { am Bitheadh sinn, um bi-u shî*gn*
         { am Bithcamaid,   um bi-u-mîtsh,
      2. am Bitheadh sibh,   um bi-u shîv,
      3. am Bithcadh iad,   um bi-ugh ĭăt.

PAST TENSE (negatively).

Sing. 1. cha Bhithinn,   { cha vi-*ign*, I could or would
                          {   not be.

      2. cha Bhitheadh tu,   cha vi-u tū,
      3. cha Bhitheadh e,   cha vi-ugh ê,
      ———— i,   ——— î,

Plur. 1. { cha Bhitheadh sinn, cha vi-u shî*gn*,
         { cha Bhitheamaid,   cha vi-u-mitsh,
      2. cha Bhitheadh sibh,   cha vi-u shîv,
      3. cha Bhitheadh iad,   cha vi-ugh ĭăt.

FUTURE TENSE (conditionally).

Sing. 1. ma Bhitheas mi,   mu vi-us mî, If I be.
      2. ma Bhitheas tu,   mu vi-us tū,
         ma Bhitheas e,   mu vi-us ê,
      3. ——————— i,   ——— î,
Plur. 1. ma bhitheas sinn, mu vi-us shînn,
      2. ma bhitheas sibh, mu vi-us shîv,
      3. ma bhitheas iad,   mu vi-us ĭăt.

INFINITIVE MOOD.

a bhi,   u vih,   to be
do bhi,   do vih,   to be

---

* Ged bhitheas mi, &c. Though I be, &c.
  Mar bhitheas mi, &c. How I may be; as I shall be, how I shall be.

le bhi,	le vih,	by being
ri bhi,	ri vih,	to be ; by being
gun bhi,	gun vih,	without being
seach a bhi,	shy̆ech u vih,	rather than be
ach a bhi,	ach u vih,	only to be [to be
los a bhi,	llos u vih,	about to be ; going
gus a bhi,	güss u vih,	going to be ; to be
gu bhi,	gu vih,	to be ; for being
&c.		

PARTICIPLES.

Past.

iar bhith,	er vih,	being ; having been
an déigh bhith,	un jeĭ vih,	{ after being ; after having been.

PHRASEOLOGY.

THE ARTICLES,

a', an, am, the.

A' is used before feminine nouns beginning with b, c, g, m, p ; and requires these letters to be aspirated.

Examples.

Orthoepy.

A' bhean,	u vén,	The woman
A' ghéug,	u ghy̆é′q,	The branch
A' mhuir,	u vüĭr,	The sea
A' phòg,	u fô′q,	The kiss.

An is used before mas. nouns beginning with a, c, d, e, g, i, o, r, s, t, u ; and before feminine nouns beginning with a, d, f, i, l, o, n, r, s, t, u.

Examples.

An ad, *f.*	un att,	The hat
An cuan, *m.*	ung cŭăn	The ocean
An dag, *m.*	un dak,	The pistol

PHRASEOLOGY.

An éibhleag, *f.*	un ĭél'ẙak,	The coal
An gunna, *m.*	ung günn'u,	The gun
An ìsp, *f.*	un î'sp,	The rasp
An òrdag, *f.*	un ôr'dak,	The thumb

The Articles.

An réis, *f.*	un ré'sh,	The race
An solus, *m.*	un sol'us,	The light
An treasg, *m.*	un tresq,	The draff
An ùpag, *f.*	un ūp'aq.	The shove.

Between the article, and masculine nouns beginning with a vowel, or feminines beginning with s,—a t,—with a hyphen, is inserted. *v. Declension supra.*

Examples.

An t-àm,	ug tânhm,	The time
An t-éud,	un tshé't,	The jealousy
An t-ìm,	un tî'm,	The butter
An t-òr,	un tôr,	The gold
An t-ùth,	un tū,	The udder
An t-sùil,	un tūïl,	The eye
An t-srad,	un trat,	The spark.

And between the article and the genitive of masculines in s. *v. ut supra.*

Examples.

An t-sìoda,	un tshî'du,	of the silk
An t-snàth,	un trânh,	of the yarn
An t-seilich,	un teïl'ich,	of the willow
An t-sùigh,	un tūïgh,	of the juice.

Am is used before masculine nouns beginning with b, f, m, p.

Examples.

Am baile,	um baïl'u,	The town
Am preas,	um press,	The bush

Am fleasgach,	um fles'cuch,	The bachelor
Am fèur,	um fê'rr,	The grass
Am measan,	um miss'an,	The lap-dog
Am mèirlcach,	um mêrr'glẙuch,	The thief.

NOUNS QUALIFIED BY ADJECTIVES.

A Gaelic adjective has only two forms; therefore there are but two genders, the masculine and feminine.

Orthoepy.

Duine math, *m.*	dü-nẙu mah,	A good man
Bean mhath, *f.*	bén vah,	A good woman
Allt cas, *m.*	ăüllt cass,	A rapid brook
Abhuinn chas, *f.*	ăü'ign chass,	A rapid river
Giulan bàn, *m.*	gẙüll'an bânhn,	A fair-headed boy
Caileag, *f.* bhàn	căigl'ak vânhn	A fair-headed girl
Còta donn, *m.*	côh'ta dŏünn,	A brown coat
Peiteag dhonn, *f.*	peh'tẙak ghŏünn,	A brown vest
Latha fuar, *m.*	lla'u fü-ur,	A cold day
Gaoth fhuar, *f.*	gû ü-ur,	A cold wind
Cù glas, *m.*	cū gllass,	A grey dog
Cearc ghlas, *f.*	kẙark ghllass,	A grey hen
Fear mór, *m.*	fèr mōr,	A tall man
Té mhór, *f.*	tshé vōr,	A tall woman
*Gnothach nàr, *m.*	gro'-uch nâr,	A shameful affair
*Saothach làn, *m.*	su'uch llân,	A full dish
*Aodach ròmach, *m.*	û'duch rrô'much,	Shaggy cloth
Mìr slàn, *m.*	mî'r sllânhn,	An entire piece
Slige shlàn, *f.*	shlik'u hllânhn,	An entire shell
Sgéula truagh, *m.*	skẙé'llu trü-ugh,	A sad tale
Bean thruagh, *f.*	bén hrü-ngh,	A wretched woman
Cnocàrd *m.*	krochk â'rt,	A high knoll
Eagluis àrd, *f.*	eq'llish â'rt,	A lofty church

---

* h is not *written* after l, n, r, though the pronunciation and perspicuity require it.

PHRASEOLOGY.

Orthoepy.

Fiamh éitidh, *m.*	fĭăv ćh'tshi,	A grim appearance
Tigh iosal, *m.*	tuïh ĭ'sh-ull,	A low house
Damh òg, *m.*	danhv ôk,	A young ox
Bròg ùr, *f.*	brô'k ūrr,	A new shoe
Daoine matha, *m.*	dû-nȳu mah'u,	Good men
Mnathan matha,*f.*	mrah'-un mah'u,	Good women
Uillt chasa,	ūïglt chass'u,	Rapid brooks
Aibhnichean casa,	ûïn'ich-un cass'u,	Rapid rivers
Giulain bhàna,	gȳüll'èn vânhn'u,	Fair-haired boys
Caileagan bàna,	căïgl'ak-un bânhn'u,	Fair-haired girls
Coin ghlasa,	cŏin ghllass'u,	Grey dogs.

MEETING.

Cia mar tha thu?	kèm'ur hâ ū	How are you?
Có so?	cō shoh	Who is this?
Có tha'n so?	cō han shoh	Who is here?
An tus' a th'ann?	un tüss'u hăünn	Is it you? [you?
Co tha leat?	cō ha lèht	Who is along with
Am beil thu beò?	um bel'ü bȳô	Are you alive?
Tha mi,	hâ mî	Yes I am
'Smath leam sin,	smaïl'um shin	I am glad of that
Gun robh math agad,	gun'-ro mah'ak-ut	I thank you
Cia mar tha iad agaibh?	kem'ur ha iăt ak'-iv	How are they with you?
Tha iad slàn,	ha iăt sllânhn	They are in health
'Smath sin,	smah shin	That's good.

PARTING.

Slàn leat,	sllânhn lèht,	Farewell
Beannachd leat,	bènn'uchq lèht,	Farewell
Soruidh uam gu d' phiuthair;	sori ü-um güt, fȳü'ir,	My respects to your sister
'Se bheatha sin,	shè vèh'u shin,	That will be welcome

PHRASEOLOGY.

PARTING.

Orthoepy.

Cuin' a thig thu rithist?	cüïn'u hik ü rih'-isht,	When will you come again?
Gu goirid,	gü guïr-rit,	Soon
'Seudar dhomh bhi falbh,	shé-tur ghoh vi fall'av,	I must be going
Tha cabhag orm,	ha cav'ak or-m,	I am in a hurry
Greas ort, ma ta,	gress orst mu tâ,	Haste you, then.

GOING TO BED.

Falbh a luidhe,	falv u llãi,	Go to bed
Cuir dhiot,	cüir yîuht,	Undress
Laidh fòil,	lluï f l,	Lie still
Dean cadal,	jén cat'tul,	Sleep
Laidh a nùll,	lluï-u-nnūll,	Lie over
Cadal math dhuit,	cat'tul mah yüt,	A sound sleep to you
Thoir leat mo bhrògan,	hoir léht mo vrôq'un,	Take away my shoes
Cuir as a' choinneal,	cüir ass'u chuïgn 'ïul,	Extinguish the candle
Cuir air mo chois trà mi,	cüir eir mo chòsh trâ me,	Put me up early
Nì mi sin.	nì mi shin,	I will.

PHRASEOLOGY.

THE HOUR.
Orthoepy.

Cia méud uair tha e ?	cu mêt ü-uïr ha è	What o'clock is it ?
Tha e aon uair,	ha è ûn ü-uïr,	It is one o'clock
Tha e dà uair,	ha è dâ ü-uïr,	It is two o'clock
Tha e tri uairean,	ha è trì ü-uïr-un,	It is three o'clock
Tha e meadhoin latha,	ha è mўèn lla-u,	It is mid-day
Tha e meadhoin oicle,	ha è mўèn ûï'chўu,	It is midnight
Tha e goirid o'n latha,	ha è guïr-rit ôn lla-u,	It is near daylight
Tha e briseadh na fàir ann,	ha brish'u nu fàïr äunn,	It is daybreak
'Se'n lath' e,	shèn lla-è,	It is daylight
Bhuail an clag,	vü-uïl ung kllak,	The bell has rung
Tha e anmoch,	ha è an'um-uch,	It is late
Tha e moch,	ha è moch,	It is early.

THE AGE.

'De'n aois a tha thu ?	dўén ûsh u ha ü	What age are you ?
Cia méud bliathn' a tha thu ?	kè mèt blўunn'u ha ü	How many years are you ?
'Dé d'aois ?	dўé tû'sh	What's your age ?
'Dé i aois d' athar ?	dўé i û'sh tah'ur	What is your father's age ?
Da fhichead bliadhna,	dà ich'ut blўunn'u	Two score years.

PHRASEOLOGY.

Orthoepy.

An sine do bhràthair na thusa?	un shin'u du vrá'ĕr na üss'su	Is your brother older than you?
Cha-n eadh : is sine mise,	chan egh : us shin'-u mish'u	No : I am older
'S esan a's òige,	shess'unn us òik'u	He is younger
Cha-n eil thusa sean?	chan ĭel üss'su shĕn	You are not old ?
Tha mi aois mhath,	ha mi ü'sh vah.	I am a good age.

THE WEATHER.

Ciod an uair a th'ann ?	cut un ü-ur̆-u hăünn	What kind of weather is it ?
Tha'n t-uisg' ann,	han tuĭshk ăünn	It rains
Tha gaoth mhór ann,	ha gŭ vŏr ăünn	It blows hard
Tha'n t-uisge trom ann,	han tuĭshk'u trŏim ăünn	It rains heavily
'S dona 'n latha th'ann,	sdon'un lla-u hăünn	It is a bad day
Nach fuar an t-side so ?	nach füi-ŭr m tyĭ-tyu sho	Is not this cold weather ?
'S olc an aimsir so,	sollehq un cin'ishir sho	This is bad weather
'S musach an uair a th'ann,	smiiss'uch un ü-ur̆-u hăünn	It is dirty weather
Tha'n latha'n diugh fliuch,	han lla-un dyü flyüch	This is a wet day
Tha e blàth,	ha ò bllá.	It is warm.

RISING.

Eirich.	é'rich	Arise
An d'éirich thu ?	un dyĕ'rich ü	Have you got up ?
Nach d'éirich thu flathast ?	nach dyĕ'richü- ha-ust	Are you not up yet ?

PHRASEOLOGY.

Orthoepy.

Am beil thu dol a dh'éridh?	um belü doll'u yié'ri	Are you going to get up?
So, so, cuir umad,	sho, sho, cüïr üm'ut	Come, come, dress yourself
Bi ealamh,	bi ell'uv	Be quick
Dean cabhag,	dўan cav'aq	Make haste
Tiucainn a shràideamachd,	tüüq'ïɲn u hrâït-um-uchq	Come to take a walk.

WASHING.

Thoir h-ugam uisge,	hoïr hüq'um uïshk'u	Fetch me water
—— siabunn,	—— shўu'punn	—— — soap
—— searadair,	—— shўaru-tèr	—— — a towel
—— cìr,	—— kï'rr	—— — a comb
—— sgàthan,	—— scâ-an	—— — a looking-glass
—— spong,	—— spōnqq.	—— — a sponge.

EATING.

Ith so,	ich or ih sho,	Eat this
Siuthad,	shўü'ut,	Say away
Fair an t-aran,	faïr'-un tar'an,	Hand me the bread
Fair dhomh ubh,	faïr ghoh üh,	Hand me an egg
Fair an càise,	faïr'-unɲ câ'-shu,	Hand me the cheese
An gabh thu iasg?	unɲ ga-ü iüsq,	Will you have some fish?
An gabh thu tuille?	unɲ ga-ü tüïgl'i,	Will you have more?

PHRASEOLOGY.

Orthoepy.

Ciod tha dhìth ort?	cut'ha yì orst,	What do you want?
Thoir dhomh spàin,	hoir ghoh spàin,	Give me a spoon
Thoir dhomh sgian,	hoir ghoh ski-an,	Give me a knife
Thoir dhomh crioman,	hoir ghoh cri:n'an,	Give me a bit.

DRINKING.

Thoir dhuinn dram,	hoir ghuign dràiun,	Give us a dram
Thoir h-ugainn siola,	hoir hū:ʒign shȳ'lu,	Fetch us a gill
Thoir h-ugainn leth bhodach,	hoir hūq'ign, gleh'vot-tuch, sho ê,	Fetch us a half-mutchkin
So e,		Here it is
Lion do ghlaine,	glȳan-du ghlluin'u,	Fill your glass
Air do shlàinte,	er-du hllàiyn-tȳu,	Your health
Sid ort,	shitt orst,	Here's to you
Slàinte dhuitse,	sllàign'tȳu ghuht'su,	Health to you
Slàint' agadsa,	sllàignt aq'ut-su,	May you have health
Tapadh leat,	tah'pu lĕht,	Thank you (success to you)
Ol as e,	ôl ass-ê,	Drink it off
Sgob as e,	scòp ass'-ê,	Cap it off.

FISHING.

Tiucainn a dh'iasgach,	tȳūq'ign-u yiŭs-cuch,	Come to fish
Thoir leat do shlat,	hoir lĕht-du hllaht,	Take your rod

PHRASEOLOGY.
Orthoepy.

Fair cuileag,	fair cüïgl'ak,	Give me a fly
So dubhan,	sho dü-an,	Here is a hook
Iasgaich an so,	füsg'ichun sho,	Fish in this part
An d'fhuair thu dad?	un dü-äir-ü dat,	Got you any thing?
An d'fhuair thu sgobadh?	un dü-äir-ü scópugh,	Did you get a nibble?
Bheil iad a' gabhail?	vel iăt-u ga-él,	Are they taking?
An do ghlac thu gin?	un du ghlachq'-ü gin,	Did you take any?
Ghlac mi bànag,	ghlachq'mi bânhn'aq,	I took a grilse
Ghlac mise tri bric,	ghlachq mish'u trî brichk,	I have taken three trouts
Cuir 'sa chliabh iad,	cüïrs'u chlÿav iăt,	Put them into the basket
Feuch am biadhuinn.	fé'ch-um bÿu'ign.	Try the bait.

SHOOTING.

Rach a shealg,	rèch'u hÿéll'aq,	Go to hunt
Fair mo ghunna,	fàir-mo ghùnn'u,	Give me my gun
Sid lach,	shitt llach,	Yonder is a wild duck
Tilg oirre,	til'ik oïr'n,	Fire at it
Thoir dhomh fras,	hoïr gloh frass,	Give me some shot
Féuch peileir,	fé'ch peïl'ér,	Try a ball
Tilg urchair,	til'ik ir'uch-ir,	Fire a shot
Tha 'n fùdar fliuch,	ham fü'tur flÿiich,	The powder is wet

PHRASEOLOGY.
Orthoepy.

An tilg mi?	un til'ik mi,	Shall I fire?
Cuir air lugh i,	cūr'-er llagh'i,	Cock it
Thuit an spor,	hūīt'un spor,	The flint has fallen
Tha 'ghlass dona,	ha ghlass don'u,	The lock is bad
So an t-slat.	sho-un tlaht.	Here is the ramrod.

SAILING.

Iomair,	ïum'ir, or im'ir	Row, pull
Fair an ràmh,	faūr'un rǎuhv,	Give me the oar
Tarruing an sgòd,	tar'rign un scòtt,	Haul the sheet
Suidh air an stiùir,	su'er-un stÿūir,	Take the helm
Càm ris i,	cūm rishí,	Keep her to windward
Thoir astar dhi,	hoïr ass'tur yih,	Give her way
Leig leis i,	lleïk leïsh'i,	Let her go before the wind
Cùm air do làimh,	cūn er'du llǎinhv,	Keep steady
Lasaich an sgòd,	llass'ich-un scòtt,	Slack the sheet
Mancuairt i,	mung cü-aïrsht-i,	About
Nuas an seòl,	nii-ass-un shÿòll,	Lower the sail
Mach na raimh,	mach'nu rǎinhv,	Set the oars
Gu tir,	gü tshïr,	Ashore!
Leig as an achdair,	yïcïk-ass' un achqïr,	Let go the anchor

PHRASEOLOGY.

Orthoepy.

Léum gu tir,	glÿém gu tshìr,	Jump ashore
Fair am ball.	fairum bàull.	Give me the painter.

QUESTIONS.

C'ainm a th' ort ?	qěn'ćm-u horst,	What is your name ?
Co leis thu ?	cǒ leshʹú,	To whom do you belong ?
Co leis so ?	cǒ-lesh' sho,	Whose is this ?
Co leis sud ?	cǒ-lcsh' shút,	Whose is yon ?
Co leis an tigh ud ?	cǒ-lesh'un tuíh at,	Whose house is yon ?
Co leis am fearann so ?	cǒ-lesh'um ferr'unn sho,	Whose land is this ?
Co leis an t-àite so ?	cǒ-lesh'un tàih'tshu sho,	Whose place is this ?
Co dha thug thu e ?	cǒ-ghǎ' húg'-ú-ě	To whom did you give it ?
Co dha bhuineas e ?	cǒ-ghǎ' vúin'-us-ě	To whom does it belong ?
'Dé bhéinn tha'n sud ?	jé vě-ign han shút	What hill is yon ?
'Dé'n loch tha'n so ?	jén lloch han sho	What lake is this ?
'Dé'm baile tha'n so ?	jé'm baìl'u ha sho	What town is this ?
Co é'm fear ud ?	cǒ-ě'm fěr ut	What man is yon ?
Co ì'n té ud ?	cǒ-ì'n tÿé-ut	What woman is yon.
Ciamar their mi ?	kem'ur hcìr' mi,	How shall I say ?
Ciamar théid mi ?	kem'ur hěit mi,	How shall I go ?
Cia as dhuit ?	kě ass' ghúht,	Whence came you ?

C'àit' a bheil thu dol?	câ-tẏu vel'u dol,	Whither are you going?
C'àite ruigeas tu?	câ-tẏu-ruĭk'us tū,	How far do you go?
An d'fhuair i e?	un dŭ-aĭr'i ĕ,	Did she get it?
An gabh sinn e?	ung gav'shign-ĕ,	Shall we take it?
Nach gabh sibh e?	nach gav'shiv,	Will you not take it?
Am fèum iad?	um fĕ'm ĭatt,	Must they?
Nach fèum mi?	nach fĕ'm-mi,	Must I not?
Am mi?	um-mî,	Is it I?
An tu?	un-tū,	Is it thou?
An i?	un-gnĭ,	Is it she?
An e?	un gnẏ̆,	Is it he?
An sinn?	un-shĭgn,	Is it we?
An sibh?	un shĭv,	Is it you?
An iad?	un-ĭătt,	Is it they?

MISCELLANEOUS PHRASES.

Coma leat,	còm'u lĕht	Never heed
Leig leis,	glẏck leĭsh	Let him or it alone
Bitheamaid a falbh,	bĭm'it-u fal'av	Let us go
Tiucainn amach,	tẏŭq'ign-u mach	Come away out
Thig astigh,	hĭk'us tuĭh'	Come (thou) in

PHRASEOLOGY.

Orthoepy.

Thigibh astigh,	hik'uv-us tuïh'	Come (ye) in
Faigh dhomh bata,	faïh ghoh bah'tu	Get me a staff
Am faigh mi deoch ?	um faïh'mi dÿoch	Shall I get a drink ?
Dean suidhe,	dÿan suï-u	Sit down
Na caraich,	na caïr'ich	Do not stir
Cha ruig i leas,	charuik'-i less	She needs not
Bi falbh,	bi-fal'av	Go
Thoir ort,	hoïr-orst	Away with you
Trus amach,	triis'um mach	Get out (used to a dog)
Am beir sinn air ?	um beïr'shign-eʒ	Shall we overtake him ?
An reic thu so ?	un rÿechk'ü sho	Will you sell this ?
Cha-n eil fhios a'm,	cha gnÿel iss'um	I do not know
Seòl dhomh 'n rathad,	shÿòll ghon ra-ut	Show me the road
'Ne so an rathad ?	gnÿè-sho'un ra-ut	Is this the road ?
'Ne so an tigh ?	gnÿè-sho' un tuïh	Is this the house ?
'Ne so an t-aiseag ?	gnÿè-sho'un tash'uq	Is this the ferry ?
'Ne so an t-àth ?	gnè-sho' un-tâh	Is this the ford ?
'Ne so an duine ?	gnÿè-sho un düin-u	Is this the man ?
'Ni so a' bhean ?	gni sho-u ven	Is this the woman ?
Trothad an so,	trò-ut-un shoh',	Come hither

PHRASEOLOGY.

Orthoepy.

Thig an so,	hik·un sholi,	Come hither
An cluinn thu?	ung cluĭṅn-ŭ,	Do you hear?
Haoi,	hû-i,	Ho!
Bi clis,	bi-clish,	Be quick
An stad mi?	un stat·mi,	Shall I stop?
Gabh romhad,	gav ronh·ut,	Go on
Gabh a null,	gav·u nūll,	Go across, (over)
Thig a nall,	hik·u nāŭll,	Come over
Rach thairis,	rach haĭr·ish,	Go across
Gabh air,	gav-er,	Beat him
Na gabh air,	na gav-er,	Do not beat him
An gabh mi air?	ung gav mi er,	Shall I beat him?
Na bi ris,	na-bi-rish,	Do not meddle with him
Dean deas,	dỹan dỹess,	Make ready
Dean deas thu fein,	dỹan dỹess ū fén,	Make yourself ready
Na h-abair smid,	na hap·ir smitsh,	Don't say a word
Na h-éirich,	na hé·rich,	Do not rise
Na h-innis e,	na higṅ·ish-è,	Do not tell it
Na h-òl deur,	na hôl dỹar,	Do not drink a drop
Na h-ùp i,	na hūhp·-i,	Do not push her

PHRASEOLOGY.
Ortloepy.

Na bac sinn,	na bachq shiṇn,	Do not hinder us
Na eumaibh e,	na cŭm′iv è,	Do not keep him, or it
Na deanaibh sin,	na dỹè′n-uv shin,	Don't (ye) do that
Na fàgar sinn,	na fà′g-ur-shiṇn,	Let us not be left
Na goid e,	na guït′è,	Do not steal it
Na lèuun air,	na glỹè′m-er,	Do not fight him, (attack)
Na mill e,	na mĭgl-è,	Don't spoil it
Na nàraich mi,	na nâr′ich mi,	Do not disgrace me
Na pillibh,	na piḷl′iv,	Do not ye return
Na leig leatha,	na gleĭk lè-u,	Do not permit her
Na riaraich e,	na rỹur′ich-è,	Do not distribute it
Na saoil sin,	na sŭĭl shin,	Do not think so
Na tairg air,	na tèr′ik er,	Do not offer for it
Farraid dheth,	farr′it yèh,	Enquire at him
Farraid dhi,	farr′it yih,	Enquire at her
Farraid dhiubh,	farr′it yŭ,	Enquire at them
Am farraid mi?	um farr′it mi,	Shall I enquire?
Nach farraid thu?	nach farr′it ŭ,	Wilt thou not enquire?
Iarr air,	ĭurr′-er,	Ask him; bid him
An d'iarr thu air?	un dỹurr′ŭ-er,	Did you bid him?

PHRASEOLOGY.

INTERROGATIVES AND RESPONSES.

There is in Gaelic no affirmative word corresponding to the English "yes," or negative corresponding to the English "no." A question is put by the interrogative form of the verb, and the answer must be made by the affirmative or negative form of the verb correspondent in tense to the form used in putting the question.

EXAMPLES.
Orthoepy.

An beil e beò ?	um beil'ò byò,	Is he alive ?
Cha-n'eil e,	cha nẏel ê,	(No) he is not
An do phòs e ?	un du fòs ê,	Did he marry ?
Cha do phòs,	chat'tu fòs,	(No) he did not
An gabh thu so ?	ung gav'ü sho,	Will you take this ?
Cha ghabh mi,	cha ghav mî,	(No) I will not
'Ne so Séumas ?	gnẏè sho shé'mus,	Is this James ?
'Sè.	shê.	(Yes) it is
'An ise bh'ann ?	un ishru vǎünn,	Was it she ?
'Si.	shî.	(Yes) it was
An d'fhàg e i ?	un dàg'è-i,	Did he leave her ?

PHRASEOLOGY.

Orthoepy.

	Orthoepy.	
Dh'fhàg,	ghàq,	(Yes) he did
Nach faodadh e?	nach fût'ugh è,	Might he not?
Dh'fhaodadh,	ghût'ugh,	(Yes) he might
Cha-n fhaodadh,	cha nût'ugh,	(No) he might not
An do thog thu e?	un'du hòq'ü-è,	Did you lift him, it?
Thog,	hòq,	(Yes) I did
Cha do thog,	chat'tu hòq,	(No) I did not
An leig sinn as e?	un gleïk'shign ass'è,	Shall we let him go?
Leigidh,	gleïk'i,	(Yes) we will
Cha leig,	cha-gleïk',	(No) we will not
Am pòs thu mi?	um pòs-ü mi,	Will you marry me?
Pòsaidh,	pòs-i,	(Yes) I will
Cha phòs,	cha fòs,	(No) I will not
An leat so?	un lèht sho,	Is this yours?
Cha leam,	cha lèüm,	(No) it is not
Is leam,	shlèüm,	(Yes) it is
An tu so?	un tü sho,	Is this you?
'Smi,	smi,	(Yes) it is
Cha mhi,	chav-vi,	(No) it is not
Co tha so?	cō ha so	Who is here? Who is this?

PHRASEOLOGY.

Orthoepy.

Tha mise,	há mish'u,	(I am) it is I
Am beil thu sgith ?	um bel'ü skî,	Are you tired ?
Tha mi,	há mî,	(Yes) I am
An òl thu so ?	un òl'ü sho,	Will you drink this ?
Olaidh,	òl'i,	(Yes) I will drink
Cha-n òl,	chan òl,	(No) I will not drink
An d'òl thu e ?	un dòl'ü è,	Did you drink it ?
Dh'òl,	ghòl,	(Yes) I did drink it
Cha d'òl,	chat dòl,	(No) I did not drink it.

GAELIC BOOKS

MACLACHLAN & STEWART,

64 South Bridge, Edinburgh.

~~~~~~~~~~

Alleine's Alarm, 18mo, bound, ...	1s.	6d.
Baxter's Call to the Unconverted, *cloth,* . .	1s.	6d.
Bible, 24mo, *roan, embossed, gilt edges,* . .	3s.	0d.
Blair's Elegy on Mr Kennedy of Redcastle, *sewed,*	0s.	4d.
Buchanan's, Dugald, Life and Conversion, and Hymns, *cloth,*	2s.	0d.
—— Hymns, separately, *sewed,* . . .	0s.	3d.
Bunyan's Come and Welcome, *cloth,* . . .	2s.	0d.
—— World to Come, or Visions of Heaven and Hell, *cloth,*	1s.	6d.
—— Grace Abounding, ...	2s.	0d.
—— Sighs from Hell, *cloth,*	2s.	0d.
—— Pilgrim's Progress, Complete in Three Parts, *cloth,*	2s.	6d.
—— Water of Life, *cloth,*	1s.	0d.
Doddridge's Rise and Progress, 12mo, *bound,* .	3s.	6d.
Dyer's Christ's Famous Titles, *cloth,* . . .	2s.	6d.
Guthrie's Christian's Great Interest, *cloth,* . .	2s.	0d.
M'Alpine's Gaelic and English, and English and Gaelic Pronouncing Dictionary, *cloth,* . . .	9s.	0d.
—— Gaelic and English Part, separate, . .	5s.	0d.
—— English and Gaelic Part, separate, *cloth,* .	5s.	0d.
M'Intyre's Songs and Poems, 18mo, *cloth,* . .	2s.	0d.
M'Kenzie's Beauties of Gaelic Poetry, *cloth,* .	10s.	0d.
M'Leod and Dewar's Gaelic Dictionary, 8vo, .	10s.	6d.

Muir's Sabbath Lessons for Schools and Families, in
    Gaelic, by Forbes, *sewed*, ... 0s. 4½d.
Munro's Gaelic Grammar, *bound*, . . . 4s. 0d.
———————— Primer, 12*mo*, ... 2s. 0d.
——— Treòiriche. or First Book for Schools, *cloth*, 0s. 9d.
New Testament, 32*mo*, ... 1s. 0d
Ossian's Poems, 8*vo*, *bound*, ... 4s. 0d.
Psalm Book, Metre, by Dr Smith, 18*mo*, *bound*, . 1s. 6d.
——— by Ross,   do. . 1s. 6d.
——— Gaelic and English,   do. . 1s. 6d.
Reid's Bibliotheca Scota Celtica, 8*vo*, *cloth*, . 6s. 0d.
Shorter Catechism, with Proofs, . . . 0s. 2d.